Tobias
and the
Angel

by
Robert Wanless

© 2002 by Robert Wanless. All rights reserved.

No part of this book may be reproduced, stored in a retrieval system, or transmitted by any means, electronic, mechanical, photocopying, recording, or otherwise, without written permission from the author.

ISBN 1-40330-136-0

This book is printed on acid free paper.

1stBooks – rev. 06/17/02

TOBIAS and the ANGEL
by
Robert Wanless

A word or two about an angel, the city of Nineveh, and the book of Tobit

The Book of Tobit is one of the literature books of the Bible. It tells of an Archangel's being dispatched to aid several good people who were having more than their share of life's difficulties. The Archangel Raphael was one of seven such beings who stand before the throne of the Almighty. The story takes in the year 681 BC, in the countries of Assyria and Media.

The story begins in the city of Nineveh, the capital city of Assyria. Nineveh had replaced the titular capital, Assur, named for the god, Assur, for whom the whole country was named, it being some seventy miles further south down the Tigris River, and where the greatness of Assyria had begun. But over the years the capital had moved up the Tigris River, some fifty miles, first to a place called, Nimrud, named for Nimrod, the great hunter and grandson of Noah. During the reign of King Sargon the capital moved again, and briefly, further north to a place called Dur Sharrukin, or Sargon's fort. Then, finally, during the reign of King Sennacherib, the capital was settled in the great and justly famous city of Nineveh. Now, in fact, it had been Nineveh from whence Assyria had been ruled for nearly two hundred years. In the opinion of King Sennacherib, Assur was more a fortress than a city, Nimrud and Dur Sharrukin even more so -- and all three too far out of the way, to boot. So Nineveh became the capital in fact.

The main duty of an Assyrian king was the making of war, war being the primary method of land acquisition, revenue and the preservation of trade routes. War for the Assyrian was something of a passion. But when passion cooled, as it always will, and the battles were over, Kings preferred cooler, more pleasant surroundings, a cosmopolitan city with its amenities, to relax in -- and that was Nineveh. There they could practice that other Assyrian passion: administration. Capital cities always draw vast numbers of bureaucrats and the others who feed off the government, all who are necessary for the running of the country, and preservation of a kingdom. These types of people, and their families, are traditionally, and conspicuously, consumers of large quantities of goods and services. In Nineveh things--all kinds of things--were plentiful and comparatively inexpensive.

When King Sennacherib rose to power, Nineveh was already one of the greatest cities of the world. He set about to complete its magnificence. He built, in addition to other public buildings, not one, but two palaces, a winter and a summer, the latter being to the east of the city and cooled, that's right, air-conditioned as it were, by the rerouting of the little Tebiltu River to join its flow to the much larger, Khosar River. The Khosar rumbled out of the Zagros Mountains and formed the south boundary of the city. Rerouting the Tebiltu drained the marshes, the "wet lands," on Nineveh's southwest side, and permitted the expansion of the city over this newly reclaimed land. This dramatically increased the size of the city, and put the Khosar right through the middle of Nineveh. The city walls were lengthened to some fifteen miles in circumference. They were strengthened too, widened to "the width of three war chariots" --nearly twenty feet across. It was an undertaking that still ranks high in the history of civil engineering.

Sennacherib had made Nineveh, in truth, an enormously large city, and one that could easily take three days to go through, as the prophet, Jonah, had protested to the Almighty when assigned by Him to give the city 40 days notice.

And Nineveh was cosmopolitan, if nothing else. It had become so in the usual ways: through agriculture, trade, and government. For many centuries it had been the major agricultural center of all of Mesopotamia. Its position on the banks of the mighty Tigris River, with its broad highway along the east side, and river traffic on it, all contributed to the city's being a trading center also. There were bazaars and markets in Nineveh offering the goods and riches of all the known world.

The great caravansary in Nineveh, a most magnificent of these invariably magnificent buildings, was a regular stop for caravans heading west, out of the Zagros mountains, from Media, Persia, Armenia, and the Indus regions far to the east, as well as the growing cities down the Tigris and Euphrates Rivers.

Caravans carried all the more portable things of the world: lumber, spices, cloth, jewels and trinkets; copper, tin, iron and other alloys. The less portable, the heavier things, the huge sculptures, enormous blocks of lime and sandstone, for building palaces, temples and public building, timber of great size for roofs and towers, were brought by river. Caravans also carried the communications between legations, government, commercial and private mail, and the "news" from distant lands, and, of course, gossip.

With this background then, you have an idea of the environment of our story, so we'll move on to the story of Tobit ben Tobiel and his family, which begins in that very city. The family Tobit had lived as captives in Nineveh for twenty years. Tobit ben Tobiel, (and for convenience sake we shall hereafter refer to him simply as Tobit) was of the family of Asiel, of the tribe of Naphtali. Our Tobit hailed from the plush upper crust town of Thisbe, which is to the south of Kedesh Nephtali, above Hazor, in pleasant upper Galilee of the Northern Kingdom of Israel.

In his native Nephtali, Tobit had been a successful merchant and administrator, which was how he and his family had been carted off to Nineveh. His native land had been conquered by Shalmanesar and it was the practice of this King, and his successors (and the later Babylonian kings, as you surely well know) to bring a good number of captives home after their campaigns of national expansion.

An area was dominated by taking the leaders, the intellectuals, artisans and professional people, to their own kingdom. These "exiles" multiplied the tribute due the conquerors considerably. The king could draw from the experience and expertise of these folks, enjoying their services far more cheaply than their native subjects. The people left behind in the captured land, farmers especially, were, in effect, leaderless, hence more docile and inclined to follow those put in charge.

King Shalmanesar, was a fair man and quick to spot talent and make use of it. And Tobit's intelligence and competence soon came to his attention. Tobit soon distinguished himself and became a purchasing agent for the King. He remained successful even later, during the reign of King Sennacherib. This position required him to travel throughout Assyria and Media, and beyond. He learned, doing so, a great deal about commodities, availability of goods, trade, and profit margins and which caravans were the better and more reliable. He learned the shipping schedules and all the myriad details that can make or break an investor. Tobit did quite well for himself.

But it was under Sennacherib that things began to go downhill for Tobit, and indeed for all the practicing Israelites in Assyria. Tobit was nothing if not resolute in his faith -- and it was that which caused his troubles. Sennacherib dared to do what his father had not done -- raid the lower kingdom of Judea and lay siege to Jerusalem. This military action, while ostensibly successful, was not as he would have liked. While he did receive tribute from the King of Judea, it scarcely made up for the cost in lives and time. Add to this that he was increasingly having trouble on both his eastern and southern fronts. He returned home in a foul humor, intent upon punishing the Hebrew people, now especially numerous in Nineveh. As usual, these remarkable people had grown and prospered in captivity. Sennacherib decreed that any Israelite who made a show of his faith was in trouble, he could be exiled farther, or killed.

Tobit's devotion to his ancient faith, particularly keeping the Sabbath and burying the dead, caused him serious problems, not the least of which was first losing his civil service position, then most of his possessions. Hearing that he had a price on his head, Tobit took refuge in a village up in the Zagros mountains. There he hid while the heat was on. This happened in the early spring of 681 BC.

Sennecherib's troubles continued to multiply and he was finally done in a *coup d'etat* led by his two sons. Then they were done in about six weeks later in still another *coup*.

When things in Nineveh had calmed down a bit, at least as far as it concerned Tobit, he came back home. Now, while he had been in hiding, with little else to occupy his time, he began to write his own story. It was several hundred years later, and a hundred or so miles down the Tigris River, in the city of Babylon, during another period of national difficulty for the Hebrew people, that someone saw in the story of this virtuous and brave man, an example for these suffering people. The story continued from where Tobit had left off, and the rest of his remarkable story was written down. Now it was told about how he went blind, and how God used one of His Archangels to help his son collect on a bearer bond and, into the bargain, rid a virtuous maiden of a demon. Topping it all off, the story told how the Archangel Raphael arranged a happy marriage for Tobit's son and the above-noted maiden. This was written down presumably in the third century BC and passed into one of the great treasures of the western world, the Holy Bible.

What we have here, then, is the rest of story, that is to say, the details filled in, the characters "fleshed out", "colorized", as it were, and the humor, for which the Jewish people are so rightly famous, restored.

Chapter 1
At the Market in Nineveh.

Tobit ben Tobiel stood patiently beneath the makeshift awning, three large pieces of canvas sewn together haphazardly and held aloft by several Ash poles shading an equally haphazard, but large, collection of bags and baskets of dried fruits, nuts and other produce. This was one of the temporary wholesale lots set up within the walls of, but outside the building, great Caravansary of Nineveh. Tobit ben Tobiel was taller than most of the Ninevite merchants haggling noisily around him. His head touched the underside of the awning. He stood quietly watching the others as they argued and haggled sometimes dramatically, sometimes just as a matter of form, as he waited to catch the attention of one of the pair of wholesalers. Tobit knew the fair market value of the commodities he sought, higher than what some of the hagglers were willing to pay, and was willing to bide his time to offer payment. Swatting at a fly on his face was sufficient, along with his height, to attract the attention he wanted. He raised both hands indicating the items, and the amount, the wholesaler nodded acknowledgement and the deal was quietly and speedily consummated. Tobit stepped to the side to pay the man. Doing so he was followed by two boys. The wholesaler eyed the money carefully, then handed over two sacks. Each sack weighed about fifteen pounds. One contained prunes and this was handed to one of the boys. The other sack was filled with Macadamia Nuts, these went to the next boy.

Tobit spoke to the boys,"...Maybe only an hour to my stand at the Hebrew Market -- four tinners each? Make it quicker and I'll give you five." he said.

"Yes sir," they replied, almost together, in Ninevian argot.

Robert Wanless

They were a pair of post pubescent boys, dusty, curly headed, dark eyed, but pleasant looking none-the-less. They were some of the numerous scabs or brats (they had other names too) who hung around the caravansaries and docks with the other day laborers, seeking a day or even an hour's work. The boys were a rough bunch of orphans, bastards, and castoffs, who, on the whole, could be counted on for a few hours grudging labor. While requiring watching, they were reasonably trustworthy, if not conscientious.

The three went on their way in the hot afternoon sun, with a distracted Tobit walking ahead. They headed first along Wall Road, the road at the base of the city wall. From the great caravansary near the Assur Road Gate, at the southwest corner of the city, they went east for a half-mile or so, turning northward with the wall. At the military foundry, Tobit turned onto Middle Road, heading north and on through a section of factory workers' barracks. On then the three walked through another section, a better one, of the homes of overseers and NCOs. It was not the best part of town. But once past these areas, he entered the Israelite section of the city. It was the newer section of Nineveh, a riverside community, by Khosar River, and on the East Side of town. While other nationalities lived in this section, it was now primarily made up of Israelites. It was they who had developed it when they were dropped there as their abode in exile, some twenty years ago.

Tobit observed that the boys seemed fairly reliable, and he walked ahead now to lead the way to his stand. Tobit had acquired the stand after he had lost his comfortable and secure civil service job. His nephew, Akihar, a mid-ranking minister in the treasury and a scribe in the royal office, had used his influence for the return of Tobit's house, and half his cash funds (the other half paid the curious "confiscatory fees" his misfortune had caused him.). Tobit used a good portion of his remaining funds to buy the stand from a widow whose husband

Tobias and the Angel

had suffered a similar fate to Tobit's, but he had not returned to Nineveh. A day spent negotiating with the widow offered sufficient reason why he hadn't returned and left some doubt as to whether the woman was in fact a "widow". Tobit paid the hundred shekels, far more than the stand was worth. He got for this what amounted to an old, well-worn tent, some weathered tables and basket stands, several tattered baskets and chipped jars and bowls. But the sale did include a modest sized, prominently placed, space in the market.

Tobit drew on his experience in buying; his acquaintance with numerous wholesalers and caravan masters, his knowledge of the various market centers and suppliers; to make sure his stand was well stocked. And it was, with fresh produce, imported fruits and nuts and spices, as well as an interesting selection of cups, jars, baskets and sacks from all over. He was a true believer in the old adage, you can't sell from empty shelves, and the presumed, corollary, full shelves a wealthy merchant make. And, sure enough, within a few months of opening the stand, once again the good man was prospering. Tobit had it in mind to make enough money with the stand to fund a ransom, and return to his homeland of Naphtali, in the Northern Kingdom of Israel.

Today was the day before the eve of Pentecost, or the feast of weeks, as it is sometimes known. He was counting on the Hebrew community, specifically those not intimidated by the unsympathetic, if not hostile, attitude of the government toward Hebrews, to do a good portion of their holiday shopping with him.

So it was that he walked along, his head down, his eyes nearly closed, the concerns for his countrymen weaving through his mind. He was in part in prayer and part in thought, each distracting the other, as he moved along briskly.

Suddenly his way was halted as he bumped into an obstruction, and heard a voice saying: "Stop, Yaudai." The obstruction was a hand stuck up to stop him, and the voice was of a curious fellow, clothed in a bulky and dirty loin skirt, his head covered with a sweaty leather cap, a foundry worker's neck shield hanging down from it and spreading to cover his shoulders. He didn't exactly look like a foundry worker. He was skinny and brown, and not the burly sort who worked the foundries. Anyway, he was leaning against the front wall of a tavern, and had put his hand out to stop the briskly passing Tobit.

Tobit had stopped short, and the boy carrying the sack of prunes, following too closely behind, and not paying attention, bumped into him. Tobit looked down, first at the hand with two of the fingers missing spread on his chest, then up into the seemingly kind eyes of the man.

Instinctively Tobit replied, "Bene Yisrael" (or "Son of Israel") to the man, distinguishing himself from a "Yaudai" (one from Judea).

The man continued speaking in a curious argot, part Akkadian, part slang, with a general salting of Hebrew words. Tobit strained to understand what the fellow was talking about and finally was able to make out, "There is a patrol coming from up the road there, where you are heading. If you and the boys slip into the tavern here I'll let you know when they are gone by."

Tobit said nothing, only nodded his head and grunted acknowledgment. He turned to the boys and with his head and eyes bid them into the tavern doorway. The boys understood and slipped quickly into it. Tobit followed easing against the wall into the shadow, and then extended his hand across the entrance in case one or both of the boys should use this opportunity to make off with the bags.

The afternoon sun was bright in the street, but casting long and dark shadows to the northeast side of the street. The constables were walking into the direct sunlight. With the

Tobias and the Angel

tavern doorway in the lee of the sun, it was dark and hard to see into from outside -- and, God knows, hard enough to see anything inside.

Tobit and the boys waited quietly, The boys began to make approving noises at the smells of the tavern and also licking their lips. Tobit cautioned them to be quiet with a threatening frown and a finger to his mouth. Outside a squad of four royal constables walked by across the street from the tavern, eying the helpful Ninevite disinterestedly. The leader was a Corporal, Tobit could tell by his dull, smooth, bronze helmet and dark, knee length tunic, trimmed in orange, and with a prominently displayed large dagger in a sheath across the front of his stomach. The other three were privates, wearing only the short leather tunic, the peaked leather cap, and each carrying a small sword in his scabbard. They may or may not, in fact, have actually have been fishing for trouble, which is to say, looking for Hebrews "making too much of display of their religion" --the way it was put when issuing a fine, or worse. But with this the beginning of a holiday season, well known by all in these quarters, the constables might well have been trawling. Anyway, an ounce of prevention, Tobit thought. And he silently gave thanks to quick thinking on the part of the Ninevite. They were often kind to the Hebrews, or Yaudians, as they called them, in such ways. In spite of being the warlike Assyrians, Ninevites were a pleasant lot. And too, it may have been a bit of an entrepreneuring; Hebrews were known to be generous in payment for such kindness.

The squad of constables, while appearing easy going, was still formidable looking. Chatting casually among themselves, they marched along their way, more or less in step, down Straight Street and out of sight. It was afternoon, and they were probably going off duty, Tobit thought.

The Ninevite gave a brief high whistle, and Tobit stepped back out of the doorway, followed by the boys. He pressed a coin into the fellow's hand, and mumbling a line or two from one of David's psalms of thanksgiving, he continued on the remaining quarter mile to his stand at the Hebrew Market.

It was not officially called the Hebrew Market, obviously. But it was known as such. And it did comparatively as much business as the market adjoining the Great Bazaar, only a mile or so to the west. Tobit's stand was the first stand to be seen when you entered the Market Square from the Great Bazaar Road. The "square" was actually a large circle, or hub, formed by the junction of several streets moving into it from various directions, including, the Great Bazaar Road and Straight Street.

The front of Tobit's stand was lined with baskets of fruit, nuts, and produce. Shelves on the side and in the back of the stand held glass jars of spices, and on the lower shelves pottery jars of oil, wheat berry and ground flour.

Sitting inside the tent, out of the sunlight on a canvas stool, was a handsome young man. He was rather tall, as was his father, and the way he sat indicated he was lanky and a bit awkward. His dark wavy hair was uncovered, and he was wearing a simple white tunic, covered with a mantle like apron, of blue and white stripped cotton twill. The bottom of this apron was turned up to form a large pocket. The young man was busily pressing a sharpened dry reed into a soft clay tablet. Seeing his father enter the tent through the opening in the side of the thick canvas wall, the boy rose in respect and happy greeting. He also reached over to hold the opening apart for the two boys who followed the older man in.

"Blessings, Son. Have you been busy?"

"Not bad I suppose." He pointed to the coins in the pocket of his apron.

"Good. All right, boys dump some of the prunes into this basket," he said to the one, "and you can put some of the nuts into this one," he added to the other. "For payment, which do you want something to eat or coins to spend?"

Tobias and the Angel

"Coins, sir."

"Coins? How about a good bunch of prunes and some wheat flour for your mother?"

"Prunes?" And they both started giggling, pointing to their behinds then holding their noses. "Please sir, and our mother has much barley already, sir."

"Coins for you, huh? To go back to that tavern and drink that sweet beer, or --"

"For our mother ... sir."

"Tobias, give each of the boys a small sack of the prunes, and, what, four tinners each?"

"Five ... sir. We have sisters at home and we are working for their dowries."

Tobit smiled wryly at the boys, speaking to his son: "We had to wait standing in a tavern while a squad of constables was on the prowl. The boys smelled the beer, and now they want to go back. Drunkenness will be the ruin of you."

"We want to be soldiers, sir, so we have to learn how to hold the drink."

"Take the pay. Trade it for beer, or give to your mother. You choose."

"Thank you, sir ..." they both said profusely, bowing sarcastically; then mumbled something about Tobit being cheap as they started out.

"Watch your tongue." Tobias said, teasing.

"Watch your own. Everyone knows what scribes do with their tongues -- and it's not wrapping them around sausages and almonds, either," said the one. And he stuck his tongue out in an obscene gesture.

"Brats." Tobias said and make a feint toward them in reply. But the boys were quickly away. The young man thought a moment about the insinuation the boys had made. It was a common enough. Most boys thought thus of scribes. The fact was Tobias wanted to be more than a scribe. Scribes were well paid, and it was a relatively prestigious profession, but hardly the profession for a young *man*. Tobias wasn't frail, or in anyway effeminate looking, he wasn't strapping, or overly muscular, either. But, he believed himself big enough and strong too. Spending the rest of his life bending over clay tablets, was not what he wanted to do. He felt he could be an officer in the army. He was smart, quick, and healthy. And even though he had never been in a fight, a serious fight (he wrestled, of course, all young men wrestled) he had never used a light sword for fencing. He often entertained, in his mind and heart, the stories of King David, and entertained fantasies at being called by The Most High, as David had been, to be an officer in an army formed for the defending his countrymen. For now, anyway, he helped his father place the bags beneath the tables holding the wicker baskets of fruit and produce. He said aloud to his father what had been in his mind: "Maybe I could stand for officer's school, father?"

"What, in the Assyrian army?"

"Well, when we finally return to our homeland, I could always draw on the training to…"

"Serve God as you can. Study the scribe, then the Law. Leave war to the warriors."

Tobit and Tobias looked up together as two men standing in front of the stand suddenly blocked the sunlight in the stand. With their faces back lighted by the sun, it was a moment before Tobit recognized them as Ahnael and his son Akihar, Tobit's brother and nephew.

"You sell fruit?" Asked the older of the two.

"Fruit? Do we sell fruit? Is this a fruit and produce stand or a hardware stand?" Then Tobit's eyes, becoming accustomed to the bright backlight, recognized both men, and said warmly: "Ah, good afternoon. And it is a good afternoon, when two such good kinsmen come to visit. Ahnael, and you too, Akihar. You've come late to the market for a bargain, I see."

"Just out for an afternoon stroll, Brother, just a stroll to get the blood circulating. And a chance happening to pass your stall as you came in -- is it to close?"

"It grows late. But as long as there are buyers there will be sellers."

"As long as there are wise sellers -- good merchants, then there will be buyers. You are prospering?"

"I've done worse."

"How is your good wife, Anna?"

"She is well, brother. And your own?

"Unwell, of course -- which is to say well. She is never so well as when unwell and well able to command the attention of one of these expensive Assyrian 'healers.'"

"Better to spend the money on Urian prunes. Here. Son, give your uncle a measure of those prunes we just received."

Tobias measured out a quantity of the prunes and handed them to the older man while his father said, "These effect an excellent physic and will make her well."

"Oh heavens, I would never hear the end of that. If she had to choose between the two I'm sure she would prefer constipation. No, let the poor woman enjoy her afflictions and attention. Now I, on the other hand, love the things and I'll take them." He tastes one. "These are delicious. Here, son, try one..."

Tobit, solicitous, quickly said to his son: "Here, Tobias, my boy, another measure for my nephew."

"For the sake of the gods, no." the younger man said. "Thank you, but they have far too great an effect on me. I'll be spending my evening and most of the night in the throne room."

"Then have some pistachios, or better still, macadamia nuts? A good year, a good crop, a good celebration of the feast." Tobit and his brother looked at each other but were silent.

"Come now, my friends, my countrymen, my very brother, you act embarrassed. These are the wonderful days for us. Our holy feast days."

Ahnael spoke softly, "Don't you think, under the circumstances; we would all be wise to be a little less obvious with the old traditions? Let us keep them in our hearts, by all means ... at least till the dust has settled ... and those rabble-rousers and Babylonian sympathizers are rounded up."

"Our young fellows are not so much rounded up as run down and left as carrion -- food for the dogs."

"They ask for it. We're permitted certain leeway in our prayers, and some of our traditions, our laws if you will ... let's leave it at that for the time being. It is after all, their country."

'That's very big of you, brother, but it isn't as if we were tourists. I don't know about you, but I wasn't exactly invited to come here. Anyway, it isn't just our religion. Esarhaddon is simply carrying on where Sennacherib left off after his losses in Judea. He's using us to make him seem tough and pay for his weaknesses. Blame the Israelites and the Babylonians, and he looks better, huh? You know he no longer controls the roads to the south or the east."

"Where have you heard such treason?"

"Treason!? Come on, Brother. Simple facts. Spend time at the caravansaries, you'll soon know every thing in the world," Tobit said.

"Well, I'd keep quiet about what I hear there if I were you, brother. Oh, we'll go home again -- and sooner than later, I'll wager. Remember, in spite of your difficulties, you've fared pretty well here."

"Well, there was that little problem," Tobit reminded him discretely.

"You caused your problems yourself, you know. And, by the way, your problems caused no small difficulty for Akihar, here."

Tobias and the Angel

"I'm certainly sorry for that. And I've never been less than appreciative for his help. But, keep in mind it was my life and the lives of my wife and son, here that were in the balance."

"It was all temporary, anyway," Ahnael reminded Tobit.

"You know as well as I the pressure is increasing on us — well upon me, anyway. Look; never mind all of this. I understand what with your position and all. So, if you can't celebrate Pentecost at your house, then perhaps you'll come to mine! Let me run the risk in giving honor to our God."

"Don't be self righteous, Brother. You continue to bring a lot of your difficulties on yourself. Let the dead bury the dead, if you know what I mean."

"That's the problem, Ahnael, they don't get buried, and our law clearly states..."

"That's just the point, Tobit, we are not living under our laws."

"No matter what the laws of the King are, God's law is always supreme."

"Fine. Tell that to the constables. It is getting late. My best to Anna."

"Shalom," said Tobit.

"Salaam," returned his brother

Tobit watched the two men, rather hurriedly move on. Watching them he looked up and saw the late afternoon sun frame the tallest tower of the distant palace. "Let's call it a day, son," and the two, father and son, without further conversation, began packing away the produce into sacks and baskets. These they loaded into their cart, and dropping the front flap of the stand, closed it for the afternoon, and together, with their hands sharing the hand rail on the cart, began pushing it as they made their way home along the dusty winding streets of Nineveh. It was not far from the market to their home in the better part of the Hebrew section.

Robert Wanless

Tobit normally looked forward to the feast days with a joyful heart, but tonight the cynicism of his countryman, his very brother, had left him with a heavy heart. It was a saddened Tobit who headed home that evening. By the time they reached their home, Tobit was in a sour mood.

Chapter 2
The Eve of Pentecost, and the Pogrom

Tobit and his son approached their house, which was on the south side of the Khosar River, not far in fact from the new, large and wonderful, botanical park. It had been built by King Sennecherib to show that even Damascus was no match for Nineveh. The park was just north of the Khosar Gate, through which, of course, flowed the Khosar River and the Khosar River Road, which ran beside the river. The river was nearly a hundred yards across at that point. This gate was one of the most impressive of the fifteen or so city gates which allowed entrance to the city through the massive city walls.

Tobit looked up again to the west and the great golden globe of the sun, dropping down beyond the plains of Mesopotamia and the distant Euphrates River, and far beyond even to his homeland. Watching this sunset, he began to feel instead of the peace, which normally accompanied a sunset, a sense of foreboding. While there was nothing particularly different about this evening, save its being the eve of the eve of a great holiday. The sun was often this golden color, perhaps not this bright. But he could look directly at it without its hurting his eyes; that in itself seemed strange. And too there just seemed a finality about this sunset. Perhaps, no probably, this uneasiness was just because of the particular feast day and the conversation with his brother.

They arrived home and young Tobias pushed the cart into the alleyway between Tobit's property and that of his neighbor. There they covered it with a large tarpaulin for the evening and walked back around to the front of the house.

The house was built right on Little Willow Road, which was just off the wide Bazaar Road which lead either to the Bazaar, or to the Hebrew market, depending, of course, upon which direction you traveled. All the property was to the back of the house. That included a small courtyard, or patio, shaded partly by an overhang of the roof from the kitchen area, a small awning attached to it, and a fig tree. The kitchen garden was just beyond, all enclosed within a garden wall about five feet high and built of adobe-like bricks, interspersed with stones taken from the garden and all held together with dried mud.

The house was constructed of basically the same materials but was covered with smoothed stucco. It had been built when Tobit was doing well in government service, and was paid for with the earnings from his investments. It was bigger than most of the houses on the street. From the front is appeared as a big white square broken only with the rectangle of the front door, a dark oak planked door, with brass fittings, opening onto the road, and simple, square shuttered windows on either side. The front half of the house was two stories, the back, one. There was an entrance foyer, or hallway, which continued back to the patio in the rear. The back part of the house was comprised of the dining area, the kitchen, and two small rooms to the rear. The dining room and kitchen were on the left side, and the kitchen stretched out to the rear of the main structure. The storage room and another, which had become a small sleeping room, adjoined the kitchen. Two other rooms, one large one small, were to the right of the hall. The sleeping quarters were on the second floor reached by stairs that went up from a space between the dining and living rooms to a balcony above. An overhang of the upper roof protected the balcony. Tobit and Anna, his wife, had the larger of the two bedrooms, Tobias the smaller.

The house was furnished with purchases from throughout the reaches of Assyrian trading. They had brought a few things with them when they were led captive to Nineveh; the rest had been bought mostly in Tobit's travels. Their furniture was simple; a nice dining room table of mountain ash, simple

Tobias and the Angel

benches of fibrous wood like rattan, with soft kapok filled cushions, small tables, and an étagère. Then there were dressers and cupboards, small tables, and chairs, all attractive, and all without being ostentatious, but still prosperous looking

Anna saw the dark look in Tobit's eyes as he came through the front door, and greeted her two men warmly, "Oh you poor dears; you look so sad. Didn't you have a good day at the market?"

Tobit said nothing, only acknowledged his wife's greeting kiss on the cheek with a brief sigh, and walked straight back to the patio where he plopped down on the wooden bench under the fig tree. He sighed again in a combination of anger and sadness.

"We did well, Mother," the boy answered, following his father and raising his eyes to heaven after kissing her on the cheek.

"Then God be thanked and praised," she said kissing him back. "But why are you so sad of face, dear?" She said following them outside.

Tobias again volunteered the answers when his father didn't: "My uncle came by and they had words."

"Let your father speak Toby." Then to her husband: "He didn't invite us, huh? Well, you didn't really expect an invitation did you? At least you invited him ... and his wife ... to feast with us?" (Anna always skipped a beat when mentioning her brother-in-law and his wife together, indicating *her* to be rather an unpleasant afterthought.)

"I invited him," Tobit finally answered. "They will not be dining with us. He thinks maybe it's a little too risky to keep our feasts right now -- he doesn't want to make any waves. The man wouldn't make waves if he was drowning -- which he is, in these fleshpots -- Goshen East."

Anna turned and walked back to the dining area. She and her maidservant, Rebeccah, an orphaned Israeli girl of about twelve, continued preparing the dinner. Anna talked to her husband from the kitchen: "Maybe if you had told him we were going to have pork for the feast he might have condescended to join us."

"You've a sword for a tongue, my dear. Be charitable. He is, after all, my brother ..."

"And Cain was Abel's..."

"They have both been a great help to us."

"Until it looked like it might cost them something. And I'll bet that eel of a son of his kept those confiscatory fees, or most of them anyway."

"Enough, Anna. I won't have our festival days ruined with hard feelings in the family. Now don't speak ill anymore of our kinsmen. I'm sure the threat of losing our own dear son would make cowards of us.

"But, would it make us Assyrians?"

"Anna!" It was not often that he put his foot down. "Now, we have a great many blessings. We have all we need. God is good to us."

"I could be more zealous, Father." Tobias added, and was cut off with his mother's:

"Not by joining those zealots, I pray!" She said, peering around the doorway with a look of horror on her face.

"No, Mother, Father. Please. I mean in keeping the laws. Not in joining the zealots. But, I want to finish my studies to make money and take you both back to our homeland. That's my goal, anyway. That and taking care of you both in your old age."

Anna joined them outside in the small courtyard to enjoy the cool of the evening. Anna changed the subject: "So now we have all these provisions for the feast. And there are just the three of us -- and old Joseph, and Rebeccah, of course."

They lounged quietly: the father and son sitting on the bench, Anna on a camel chair in the shade of the Fig tree, and

Tobias and the Angel

Rebeccah silently sitting on a stool near the kitchen. The girl sat quietly, periodically sneaking shy and adoring glances at young Tobias.

Everyone sat quietly, eating pieces of spiced fried bread and drinking sweet wine. Tobit's old servant, Joseph, joined them. After a while Joseph broke the silence and began talking about seeing the sun set this afternoon over the land of Naphtali, in the mountains above Jerusalem. Tobit listened quietly to his old servant, and friend, thinking that he must have had the same reaction to the sunset, and of how almost prophetic he sounded now. Tobit listened to the old fellow talk as he watched the swallows, which nested in the garden wall, returning to roost for the evening. With it all, he thought, just as the Almighty provides for these swallows in the wall, so He provides for and protects our family.

*   *   *

The next day was the eve of Pentecost. It was reasonably busy at the stand. Tobit greeted his customers cheerfully, trying to seem optimistic, and wanting to share the spirit of the holidays. He had reduced his prices, cutting dangerously close his profit margin, mostly in charity to help others. He thought too that reducing the prices may encourage those to buy more than they might otherwise be able to afford, and reduce his inventory. He was nervous in his business projections however. Even though it was one of the three great feasts of his people, few spoke of the holiday. And there weren't as many customers as he had expected. Those who came did buy a lot, but they seemed to do so almost surreptitiously. Tobit welcomed each of the purchases, thanking and praising his customers. But, throughout the day the memory of the yesterday's conversation with his brother, and the subsequent one with his wife, kept coming into his mind. It became an effort to stay cheerful. At the end of the day, when tallying up, he was disappointed. He had expected better sales. It would be then, he determined, only a modestly celebrated feast among the practicing Hebrews.

Again, as the late afternoon sun sank to frame the highest cupola of the Palace of the King's Wives, the two, father and son, repeated again, the ritual of closing the stand. They were more thorough and careful closing for the Sabbath. It would be a whole day, before they would return. The merchants hired a guard for the Sabbath weekend, but they still took precautions. Old Joseph joined Tobit and Tobias in the afternoon, and he helped them putting most of the produce, the glass jars, and many of the better baskets, onto the cart to take home with them.

This cart bears mention: Old Joseph built it. He had bought a pair of damaged chariot wheels and a badly bent axle from one of the military repair shops. He straightened the axle himself, and adapted the wheels to fit it. He designed a curious suspension system made from two flexible iron strips, which looked like bows. These he welded to the axle. He had built a simple flat box of Zagros pine, attached it to the springs with rivets. Two simple oak beams extended out from the box, between which he inserted a handlebar of smoothed and oiled rattan. The old man had done a fine job. It was a handy cart, quite attractive, and the envy of most of the other stand owners. It had cost next to nothing and was known as Tobit's chariot. It was destined for sadder and greater loads in the days to come.

The sun seemed to wait above the distant horizon until the two men arrived home. They carried the goods from the stand to the back yard and rested them on the wall. Old Joseph lifted them down into the yard. The sun had set as they finished, and they went into the house to wash and prepare for dinner. Old Joseph prepared and helped with the ritual washing of hands and face made all the more elaborate because of the feast day. Then the three men stood quietly as Anna prepared the candles, and Rebeccah was allowed to light them.

Tobias and the Angel

Tobit surveyed the room, the table, those for whom he was responsible, and suddenly stopped the girl, as she was about to apply the lighted wick to the candle. Turning to his son, he said, "Tobias, my boy, we have so much from the bounty of the Almighty and so few to share it with. Let us remember the poor, and those who have nothing. Go out, Son, and see if you can find any poor man, or poor widow, one of our captive people, who is mindful of God, but without the wherewithal to celebrate, and bring him to share our dinner. We will wait for your return."

"Oh for heaven's sake, Tobit, Wait! It will all get cold. Couldn't you have thought of this sooner? I mean, I'm happy to share with the less fortunate, and I would gladly have delayed the spreading of the table -- but now is hardly the time..."

"I'm sorry my dear. It 's either the abundance of our blessings, or maybe my increasing age; but I think my sense of charity is dulling. Better this delay than not sharing at all. The boy won't be long."

"Oh for heaven's sake. Rebeccah, give me a hand with the meat and the soup." The good woman mumbled as they carried the food stuffs back to the kitchen, "Well, I suppose it's better than not to help some humble, poor and needy" and from the kitchen Tobit heard: "and better than what we might have had to share our meal with." She added, almost out of hearing: "I wouldn't want to have celebrated Pentecost listening to Ahnael's wife chant her litany of aches and pains, and the erotic healing ideas of her Assyrian physicians." Tobit didn't try to correct his acid-tongued wife again. Tobias went out to do his father's bidding.

The boy hadn't been gone ten minutes when he suddenly rushed back into the house, nearly out of breath and saying: "Father, there is one of our people lying murdered at the square near the junction of Bazaar Road. I think it happened just before I got there. He looks familiar. I think I know him from school."

"They are at it again. Oh for the return of Shalmanesar. First they stopped, or tried to stop, our Sabbath, now, I know, they are going to try taunting us with our burial practices -- the beasts! Anna, have your girl fetch some winding cloth. Joseph ... oh never mind, you'd better make sure we can get through the garden gate. We'll take him to the shed. The girl can leave the cloth there. Let's go son. We'll bring the lad back and bury him tonight when it's dark."

"Tonight! Oh, Tobit. God have mercy on the poor fellow, but, really, I mean -- what about our feast!"

"My dear, please. It will be dark soon. We will bring him here, hide him in the garden shed, until later. We can try to enjoy our feast, and then when it's safe, we'll bury the poor fellow." The two, father and son, quietly and quickly, slipped out of the front door to rush to the Square in the deepening dusk.

Joseph went out to the garden shed to make room for the body. He moved cuttings and pots from in front of the garden gate. This was not so much a gate as several thick pieces of wood, stuck in the ground, and held upright by two branches inserted in the top of the wall and stretched across, in front of and behind the boards. It was rarely opened, but Joseph opened it now so the body could be brought directly to the garden, instead of through the house.

Tobit had left his dinner untasted; mumbling as he walked along a prayer or oath, that he would not break his fast till he had found the body, and carried it home thence to bury it secretly when it was dark. He and Tobias walked down the street, keeping in the shadows, as he tried to recall the exact words of the laws regarding this activity. He also began to be concerned that the murdered fellow may be some kind of bait in a trap. If this was a new pogrom starting up he was going to have to be more careful this time. He couldn't afford another hiding -- even if he was able to escape. He would have to consult with the Rabbi after Sabbath prayer tomorrow about what he would be doing if or, more likely, when, things got worse.

Robert Wanless

Chapter 3
The Pogrom and the beginning of Tobit's test

The sun had set when they reached the Square, but in what was left of daylight they saw the body immediately, lying against the wall of the pool in the center of the Square. He was a strapping boy of about twenty and looked as though he had been hit from behind and pushed. As Tobit and his son knelt by the lad, they noted he was still warm; and he seemed at first to be asleep, except his head lay in an odd way, turned to the side, and looking down almost facing to his rear. His neck was swollen; it was broken. His eyes were still open and the expression on his face was of a mild surprise. Tobias said he did know him from school. He had thought the fellow was ill fitted for scribe school and would be better suited for officers' school. The two men struggled with the body of the youth getting him to his feet. He was heavy. They half carried half dragged him home. Walking along they pretended to talk to him. With his head down it might seem as though he was just drunk and hardly able to walk. When they got to the house Joseph was there by the alley to greet them and helped them down the narrow walkway between their yard and the neighbor's, to the garden gate. Anna and the girl came out and helped as they lay the boy in the garden shed. Rebeccah looked at him searchingly, saying softly, "He is very handsome."

Anna was scarcely able to hide her tears, and whispering softly "Shhh. The poor boy, the poor boy."

They closed the shed door and walked back to the house. Anna, still softly weeping, said to Tobias: "Toby, dear, do you think we can we find his mother? Suppose she is a widow and he her only support?"

"I thought he was an orphan, but I'll ask around tomorrow, and when I return to school, Mother."

The whole family, including the servants, washed carefully in the fresh water Rebecca had brought, then they all sat down to a sad and anxious meal. They began their feast quietly each person thinking of the guest hidden in the garden shed.

"How are we supposed to have a merry feast under these circumstances?" Anna asked.

Tobit mumbled: "Your feast-days shall end in lamentation and sad thoughts."

"The words of the prophet Amos, Father?" Asked Tobias.

"That they were," the older man acknowledged, sadly nodding his head.

Later that night, with the moon rising full and high over the distant mountains to the east, the three went out to bury the body out beyond the walls of Tobit's property.

Their neighbor, Hanian, who had heard the commotion between the houses earlier, kept an eye out until they came out again. He watched as the three men went about their task of burying the poor lad. Hanian was an Israelite, and an accountant in the government service,

"You're an old fool, Tobit," He said, softly as they walked by him. He was short and had to stand on a couple of stones to see over the wall. "You've had the death sentence passed on you once for such doings, and you had to run away when they were hunting for you."

"Good Sabbath, Hanian. Out enjoying the evening? No one to share the feast with? Tobias, why did we not think of inviting our neighbor?" Tobit smiled at the older man, a prim old widower.

The man was undaunted by the subject changing: "They were going to put you to death for this very thing. You were just barely reprieved, and here you are back burying the dead again! You'd better keep the king's law."

"Fear God much, and the king little."

Tobias and the Angel

"Aye, and the tax man most of all," added Old Joseph, nodding pleasantly at the neighbor.

"But all the same," Hanian continued, "fear the king, especially when he's doing works of mischief. We're not dealing with old Shalmanesar here, you know --and it's not like the old Pharaohs, either."

"It's the same principle."

"Aye, the killing of our people. But unlike old Pharaohs, we all get on well here. The only problem is these damnable rabble-rousers, and zealots like you. That's the only cause of trouble. Let them be. Bide our time and this new king will go the way of the others, some insurrection or other will take the heat off us…

"Oh go about your business, Hanian," Tobit finally said, regretting immediately being sharp and discourteous. Never make an enemy of a neighbor -- especially an old busybody of a neighbor.

"Well, it's my business if looking for you they hunt me down, too!"

"No fear of them accusing you of being a *bene Yesraeli*," Tobias added, in the Akkadian dialect.

The neighbor continued chattering on while the three men moved on to the back wall to get on with the sad work.

* * *

The death of that young man on the eve of Pentecost was indeed the beginning of a new pogrom. This was a subtler pogrom, rather reflecting the attitude of the new king. While nothing official was promulgated to raise the ire of the Israelites, and risk a troublesome insurrection, the killing was on, nevertheless. Two laws of the Israelites were thorns in the Assyrian side: keeping the Sabbath, and burying the dead. The first, because the Assyrians believed it showed incipient laziness in the Hebrew people. The second, because the bodies left to dogs or birds had always seemed a particularly effective, if unsanitary and smelly, method of making a point. Both laws interrupted work, and deprived some god or other the flesh carried "on high" by birds of prey (or dogs). And they were two things the Yisraeli people, on the whole, were particularly loath to give up and much harder to hide.

The other evidence of their nationhood was rather easy to keep muted. To reduce conflict, and to save their skin, many of the men kept their ear locks safely tucked beneath their linen caps. Traditional greetings were made more subdued. Almost everybody tried to seem as "Assyrian" as possible.

Throughout the centuries Hebrew humor has been like a surgeon's knife, aiding the soul by cutting off the epidermis of sham and pretense hiding the muscle of truth beneath. So the admonitions to act "Assyrian" were especially annoying to the young of the devout families. At first this may seem odd, since so many of them had been born in captivity and were, socially, at least, almost Assyrian. But the young rarely miss a chance to protest. This lead to an increase in black humor; it was from among the young that the jokes first started and spread. "How do you act like an Assyrian?" They began:

"Spread paint on your face and eat a pig."

"Get three wives -- and have their daughters" was another,

"Don't wash just wear more perfume." -- "Try and count the Gods" and so on.

This wasn't just youthful protest for the sake of protest; it was they who were routinely being cut down and left for dead. The presumption of the constabulary was that all the young were among the Young Zealots, or Rabble-Rousers.

It became common knowledge that anyone caught trying to bury the victims would meet a similar fate, or at least have to beat a hasty path up into the Zagros.

It also became common knowledge, at least within the exile community, that Tobit, his son, and their servant, had become

Tobias and the Angel

semi-officially those who had been burying the murdered *bene Yisraeli*. In Hebrew circles the fear was expressed that this knowledge might spread. And it became common for someone to come to the stand, look directly at Tobit or his son, and whisper a location, "By the tavern on Straight Street" and slip silently away. At night there might be a knock on the door with someone telling of another murder and where. The three men continued to steal away the bodies hide them in the shed, or behind the stand, and then, at dead of night, bury them.

After awhile Tobit began to get nervous and suspicious, lest one of the messengers prove to be setting a trap. The fear that they would arrive at a given location to find not a murdered Hebrew youth, but a platoon of constables waiting with shackles, became constant. To these fears the continuing taunting of a couple of neighbors was adding to the emotional difficulties of the situation. Would the taunts turn to out and out betrayal?

One night they were treated to some curious inverted logic: Chuz, a fellow stand holder who lived two doors down from Tobit, appeared in the field behind Tobit's house as they were burying a murdered youth: "They are only killing these fellows because you're burying them, Tobit, you fool. If you stop burying them they'll stop the killing."

"That doesn't make a whole lot of sense, Chuz. Unless you want to go to the palace, or the constabulary headquarters and negotiate some kind of settlement. Our laws say we are to bury the dead. If there were no dead, then I wouldn't have anyone to bury, now, would I?"

Chuz persisted: "But they are only doing it because you are burying them."

Tobit continued to dig, adding, "Shouldn't you be off somewhere saying your prayers?"

"Well, it would be a great evil if your actions were to bring trouble on us all."

27

"I'll give you that. Good night."

Old Joseph quietly said to Tobit after Chuz went on his way: "I think we are asking for trouble if we continue to bury here. We should find another spot."

"You're right, old friend. But where?"

*   *   *

In discussing potential graveyards with a particularly devout Rabbi, the botanical gardens came up. Now it had happened that King Sennacherib, after a sortie in Damascus, saw and was delighted by the botanical gardens there. Such gardens were common in Damascus. Sennacherib believed that the richer soil, and better climate of Assyria, such gardens would do well in Nineveh. They would be a welcome addition to the magnificence of the city he was well on the way to making one of the most magnificent the world had ever known.

He hired architects and landscapers and set about to design and have built, or planted, the greatest botanical garden anywhere. He had a new gateway built into the city walls near where the Khosar River entered the city, to aid in the building of the park. He had removed hundreds of homes, and barracks, then had trees and shrubs brought to Nineveh from all over and had them planted in the area. There were hills, and knolls, paths and ponds, and large grassy areas, a profusion of roses were brought up from Babylon; hibiscus, gardenias, lilies in incredible variety and profusion, and a wide variety of palms. And sure enough, the park was soon regarded as one of the cities greatest attractions and treasures. The garden was in the east section of the city, and the new gate was called the Khosar Gate.

Tobias learned from a particularly devout Rabbi, that not far from the Khosar Gate and just beyond the city wall, was the main nursery area where gardeners started and developed seedlings and from which they took compost and soil for the

Tobias and the Angel

botanical garden. The Rabbi suggested to Tobit that it might be a good place to bury the dead should the pogrom continue-- which it did.

They had begun to use the stand cart as a hearse to transport the dead. They filled sacks loosely with grain chaff and nut hulls, straw, or whatever, to cover and disguise the poor cargo they were now transporting. Joseph would also bring cuttings and pruning from their own garden as an excuse for bringing them to the nursery. It worked as a ruse to get them in and out of the utility gate without trouble. Soon the three men began carrying the bodies there at night. Just beyond the nursery area, over a knoll, where it was hard to be seen, and not likely to be discovered, they carefully buried the corpses.

By now it was late summer and the heat was adding to the strain of the sad activities. Long days in the stand were heaped on long nights burying the dead. Gradually the killings decreased, but the two or three extra nights each week were still more than enough. One particularly hot night the three men returned home from their labors. Tobit showed such signs of strain this night that Anna thought he might be pushing himself to death.

Anna was constantly afraid for her men folk. Since the pogrom, as nearly as it could be understood, was directed at young men, this meant her beloved son. But this night, looking at both men as they came in, she had a double fear. Old Joseph, a good deal older than the other two, had become little more than a lookout and shovel bearer -- not unimportant tasks, to be sure, but, this meant Tobit and his son were doing most of the hard work. So as Tobit came to bed that night, Anna swallowed her worst fears, and tried to comfort her husband, but not without the usual expressions of concern: "You're wearing yourself out, my dear. You are doing the work of a young man and you're not in any shape for such work. Please, for the love of God, don't make me a widow."

"I'm strengthened for and by the task."

"You couldn't prove that to look at you. Please, dear, come rest next to me." Anna gently touched her husband's back with her soft smooth hand -- it was simply too hot to embrace him.

He sat on the edge of the bed, sighed deeply and then just stared out into space. He was so tired he began to speak absently "our good son is a great help, as is old Joseph, of course. But my dear, it isn't just the digging and carrying that is making me so weary -- it's not the sadness and injustice -- it's the heat."

"It has been hot, but no hotter than usual."

Tobit went on," it's in weather like this I miss our home. It was always temperate there, up in the mountains."

"Nonsense. I remember differently. You complained of the heat there."

"Only in the summer."

"Silly man, that's the only time it's hot."

He lay down next to his wife, and she tried to comfort and encourage him. But after almost an hour of fitful effort, he still couldn't get to sleep. Finally he said, "I'm going to take some cushions and see if it is any cooler outside."

"What if it rains?"

"Then it will be cooler still. I'll sleep by the garden wall; then, when the morning sun comes up, I'll still be shaded. Don't wake me in the morning. The boy can open the stand up himself."

They bid each other good night, kissed affectionately, and then Tobit eased his way quietly and carefully down the stairs. Out in the garden he made his bed at the base of the garden wall resting his head on a thick clump of grass growing out of the foundation of it. Sighing deeply he quickly fell asleep.

In the early morning the swallows, nesting in the wall, began the daily routine of bringing food to their young. Tobit slept in the cool shade of the wall. As he slept warm droppings of guano fell from the swallow's nest in the upper part of the wall, and into Tobit's eyes. At first this didn't awaken him, but only irritated his eyes. Unconsciously, being still asleep, he began to rub his irritated eyes with his hands. This, of course, rubbed the guano into his eyes, and they began to sting. He awakened then with a start, sat up shaking his head and rubbing his eyes, startled and confused. He wasn't able to ascertain immediately what the substance in his eyes was. But hearing the birds, and feeling and then smelling the stuff on his hands, he became almost rigid when he realized what had happened. He called out for his wife:

"Anna! Anna, my dear, can you come and help me?"

Anna Answered from the kitchen: "What is it, Dear?"

"Bring me a cloth and some water. I can't see anything."

"What do you mean?"

"I mean, that I cannot see -- something has happened to my eyes and I think that I am ... blind!"

Anna rushed out to the garden with Rebecca and together they helped him up. "Oh how ugly," she said as she began wiping the mess from her husband's face. "What have you done?"

"My dear, it wasn't I who did this. I believe it was the birds that infest our garden wall."

The washing didn't help. He still couldn't see. Rebeccah and Tobias, who had joined them, helped Tobit to stand up and began leading him to the back door of the house.

Their neighbor, Hanian, suddenly stuck his head up over the garden wall and said," Blind are you! See, I told you you were a fool for all your pains. Now God has punished you for the risks you have taken."

"Nonsense. God does not punish for good works," Tobit said with conviction and a supremely irritated tone in his voice.

"Humph! Well even if He doesn't, where have all your good works gotten you? Was this the reward you had hoped for when you gave alms, and went around burying those dead ones? You've just made things difficult for all of us."

"I expected no reward for the acts of kindness I did. They are the obligations of the law, from Moses; laid down for our well being and I did only that, nothing more."

"And a fat lot of good it got you," the man added as he turned and walked away.

"The old viper," Anna mumbled as she aided her husband through the doorway.

Chapter 4
Later, In Nineveh

After several days' rest and in the expectation that the condition of his eyes would heal by itself, Tobit finally went back to work at his stand. At first he did a brisk business -- sympathy business as it turned out. Old Joseph would escort Tobit to the stand in the morning. In the afternoon either Joseph or Tobias would escort him home again. But it was becoming increasingly futile. He wasn't able to see the various items he was buying, although his sense of touch, and reputation for being fair and wise, kept wholesalers from taking advantage of him. He tried to teach Old Joseph some of what he knew, and he did help, in bringing stuffs from the markets. But this wasn't the thing for which the good man was suited. He was used to working with his hands, and he was a slow learner of the mercantile arts. So in spite of his efforts he proved a poor merchant. And in truth he was getting too old for much lifting.

Tobit had also decided that rather than pushing his son into helping more at the stand, he should be more vigorous in his studies. And although the boy came to the stand after school, he did so while continuing his appeals to attend officers' school. He pointed out that lieutenants made a good starting wage in the Assyrian army. His father reminded him that it was predicated on what was confiscated from victims. How much had their old home in Naphtali contributed to some young lieutenant's income? So, not to cause any more grief, he honored his father's wishes both by studying hard and by helping at the stand in the afternoons, and saying nothing more about officers' school.

Now, in addition to the difficulties mentioned above, it was soon obvious that the exile community had, after the initial "sympathy business" begun to give Tobit a wide berth. It was a combination of two things: pragmatism -- they feared seeming too close to him, perhaps potential associates or sympathizers if a pogrom heated up again; and this was hardest to take: there was this layer of superstition just beneath the surface of even the most enlightened Hebrew. Tobit had heard that some countrymen entertained the Assyrian superstition that the "gods" of Assyria (and there were many of them, so how could one be sure which) had looked with disfavor on Tobit for following the God [singular] of Abraham, Isaac, and Jacob. It was they or one of them anyway, which had struck Tobit. "Nonsense!" Tobit exclaimed when being told of this, "It was no Assyrian god that did this to me. It was the birds -- their droppings, only that, nothing more."

Then there was this last insult: Chuz got word to Tobit that he was right: Tobit had stopped burying the dead (because of his blindness) and the killings had, in fact, stopped.

Ahnael's wife, having heard of Tobit's "condition", couldn't avoid a condescending visit to Tobit and his family. She arrived on the scene, in a sedan chair, dressed in an elaborate gown of tiered and tasseled silk, which wound its way up from floor to waist, taking several turns in the doing. Her shirt was thick brocade, of gold and silver bonbon flowers, on an ivory field. Over this was black cloth apron, with pockets containing sweetmeats and tidbits to eat, a vial of some fragrance, a compact of facial paint, and a plethora of gold and silver coins. At his sister-in-law's insistence, and with Anna accompanying them, Tobit went, through (or down) the hierarchy of Assyrian medical practitioners.

He began consultations with an expensive *Baru*, "'a divine diviner,' as his sister-in-law described him, with her eyes raised to the regions from which the *Baru* had presumably descended. This "wise man" listened intently as Tobit explained how the "occasion" had happened. The man listened intently and said

Tobias and the Angel

very little, only nodding sagely. Finally he addressed the sister-in-law and referred Tobit to a somewhat less expensive, and even more enigmatic, *Ashipus*.

The next afternoon she appeared again and took Tobit to the *Ashipus*. This man displayed all the trappings of an out and out sorcerer: a scarlet robe, an abbreviated face mask, noxious incense, and while he displayed a mastery of spoken Hebrew in speaking to his assistant and Tobit's sister-in-law, he spoke not at all to Tobit. He complained as they were leaving, of Tobit's "hostility" and unbelief. In the course of the next couple of weeks they saw several others. The consensus of their findings was that the cause of this or that illness or condition was the displeasure of one or more of the various gods. It was more than Tobit could take. Each healer charged a handsome fee, whether he gave advice or medicine, or both. Tobit's reserves were dwindling and finally he refused to see anymore of these "false prophets, these priests of Baal," as he called them.

His sister-in-law, nonplused, and still determined that Tobit would be healed, and his healing ultimately attributed to her, thought a few moments, and after a silence rare for her, said, "Well, I know of one or two more Asu, that's physician to you, that I have not seen. But, really, Tobit, when you're in Nineveh you do as the Ninevites do. Remember, brother-in-law, these people have been treating illness as long as our Hebrew Physicians have."

Not wanting to rile further this formidable woman, he agreed to see what turned out to be three more. Their consultations, and the various salves and unction they prescribed to override the "divine displeasure," were expensive, smelly, and worthless.

After a long discussion with his brother, and the need to respect his brother's wife, Tobit agreed to see one more. This fellow practiced in a fashionable area near the Great Bazaar. He was a smartly dressed "physician-priest" in an expensively and gaudily decorated room. He gazed for a long time into Tobit's eyes, which he had propped, open, painfully, with reeds. He, of all the ones Tobit had seen (and he proved to be the last one) seemed almost to know what he was talking about. In spite of the big show of dress and office, he was a friendly chap, and rattled on, in barely comprehensible Hebrew, in spite of Tobit's reminders of his Akkadian fluency, with a breath heavy with the smell of garlic. At the end of his examination he diagnosed Tobit's condition as cataracts and solemnly pronounced it incurable, adding it was probably caused by offending the goddess of light.

The end result was that, in paying the Assyrian healers, those men and women, the cream of the crop of the Nineveh Medical Society, Tobit's savings had been wiped out. The income from the stand was now hardly enough to support the three of them, much less the two servants. Of course Old Joseph would stay on nonetheless, and Rebeccah was, for all intents, all but adopted. So the blindness continued in spite of Tobit's prayers or even, finally, his Jobian resignation.

Anna joined, at the suggestion of a friend, the army of ladies who worked for people like the Family Zinecherboels'. These were people in the cloth business. They were an outgrowth of the cotton industry rapidly growing in and around Nineveh. Cotton had been introduced into the area during the early days of Sennecherib as a cash crop. It was so successful that it spawned the cotton business and this, in turn, clothes manufacturing. Families such as Zinecherboels' bought, prepared, or actually made cloth. They bought not only the locally produced cotton yarn, but imported other yarns, wool, silk, linen, and assembled it into bolts. These bolts were then shipped by caravan on to dressmakers in Anatolia, Damascus, Palestine, and even Egypt and beyond, not to mention also being sold to the sizable population of dressmakers and tailors in Nineveh.

The family Zinecherboels was made up of a widowed mother, her mother-in-law and two daughters, who had managed to persevere in developing a limited trade at first, but before long were hiring others to provide for the ever widening demand for the cloth they wove, dyed, and assembled.

Zinecherboel's husband had been among a wave of captives from Shalmanessar's earlier raids into Palestine. The old man had ended his days sadly, a heavy drinker and heartbroken (the widow liked to lament) at separation from the land of his fathers. That a tavern brawl had resulted in stopping his heart was the more generally accepted account. Nevertheless, Zinecherboel's widow tried to keep the Sabbath and most of the dietary laws and enjoyed some prosperity.

Women were hired for the work because they could work in their homes, and their delicate hands and fingers were more suited to the tasks. It was generally easy work but terribly monotonous, and if it didn't pay well it was better than nothing. Occasionally, employers came upon the realization that being fair to the workers often resulted in better work and a modicum of loyalty. The Zinecherboels were among those few who understood this simple human concept.

The Widow Zinecherboels had sought out Anna, when the difficulties of poor Tobit became widely, but quietly, known. Anna, in spite of Tobit's protestations, decided to try the work. She was lent a loom and would weave at home. "When I deliver the cloth I am paid by the piece," she said excitedly to her less than enthusiastic husband. "With this, and with the income from the stand, and if I can continue to work hard, I can feed us well, at least until Tobias can aid us with his labor."

"God's will be done," said Tobit -- in that grudging way of those who suffer. "But I've been thinking of selling the stand, or maybe just give it to old Joseph. It makes barely enough to give us a profit."

"Humph! And then what would you do? Sit around here sulking is all you would do. No, the stand is something for you to do. It still makes a profit, even if it is a small one. Anyway, perhaps one of their physicians will come up with a salve to heal you. I saw Ahnael's wife, and God knows, no one sees more physicians than she, and she said that..."

"Paying the physicians is one of the reasons we are out of money."

"Burying the rabble-rousers is the another."

"Anna, please. The boys were only zealous. They are more to be admired than thought ill of."

"And in the end buried."

"That's true for us all."

"Leaving behind weeping mothers and widows," she added.

"What's that noise?" Tobit asked hearing the sound of a kid coming from the back yard.

"What noise?"

"That! That is a kid, is what that is. Where did you get that? Why wasn't I told about it?"

"You weren't told about it because we just got it this afternoon. It was given me by Mrs. Zinecherboels. She is very kind."

"No one gives a kid away, in a city. Give it back to her. It never shall be said that we ate stolen food or soiled our hands with theft!"

"What did you say?" The old fire, always just beneath the surface of the good woman, suddenly flared. "What are you talking about? You are accusing me of stealing! I did not steal it! It was given me as I said. The Widow Zinecherboels knows of your many kindnesses and how you have suffered for them. She sought to bring relief and comfort to us during this time of trial."

He realized she was telling the truth and said, "I'm sorry."

But she wasn't about to stop, "Fine talk that is, accusing me of stealing! Of all the nerve!"

Tobias and the Angel

"I'm sorry. I didn't ..." but he didn't get to finish. Anna was off and running:

"All your hopes and acts of kindness -- they were all false, all a pretense. You hypocrite. It was all a big show! 'Look what a good Hebrew I am!'" Her face had become red, and her normally rather soft-spoken low voice was becoming as shrill as a shrew's. "That's the reason God sends us adversity, so that he can see what we're really made of! What have you to show for all your alms giving? Huh? Look at you!"

The good but sword-tongued wife stormed out of the house. As usual, it seemed, she had given a legitimate, albeit alternative, interpretation of the situation. Tobit sighed with the universal sigh of those whose burdens are all but crushing.

The family ate in silence that night. Tobias attempted once or twice to start a conversation, but failed. He recognized the tension, and even felt guilty for having perhaps contributed to it. After dinner Rebeccah cleaned up, Old Joseph went out to his shed, and Anna went to her room. Tobias stayed with his father for a while, to see if his presence would relieve his unhappiness. It didn't. He went up to his own room to turn in for the night.

When he heard Rebeccah settle in for the night in her little berth off the kitchen, Tobit managed to fumble his way out into the courtyard.

He sat quietly on the bench beneath the fig tree. It was cool out now and a gentle breeze wafted over the darkened yard. His heavy heart and sagging spirits had left the poor man sapped of will. Finally, and with what was left of his strength, and with eyes wet with bitter tears, he prayed.

Lord, Thou hast right on thy side;
No award of thine but is deserved,
no act of thine but tells of mercy, and of justice.
Lord consider my case.
O Lord, leave my sins unpunished, my guilt,
and the guilt of my parents forgotten.

Robert Wanless

> *We are doomed to loss, to banishment and to death;*
> *Thou has made us a by-word and a laughing-stock*
> *in all the countries to which thou has banished us.*
> *It is because we have defiled thy commandments;*
> *and it is fitting punishment for the men*
> *who have neglected thy bidding*
> *or were only half-hearted followers of thine.*

> *"Now Lord; do with me according to thy will,*
> *Give the word, and take my life to thyself in peace;*
> *for me, death is more to be preferred than this life.*
> *It is better to die than bear these reproaches,*
> *than bear the shame,*
> *and the suffering of my dear wife and son.*
> *Grant, I beg you oh God, death to me,*
> *and take me to thyself."*

Tobit sat quietly and alone for a moment; there was a distant mournful call of an owl, the pleasant chirping of night creatures. He reconsidered the enormity of the request he had made. He thought of leaving his beloved Anna, a widow. Then he thought of the sadness that his death would cause his fine son. What a great gift of God the boy had always been. They had always been so close, always, so close.

But now his life had become a burden to others. And, of course, all life must end anyway. It was sad, it was tragic even, that his must end in exile, away from the burial grounds of his father, his fathers' father, of all his fathers before him, back to Abraham. He sighed again and moved his hand to his eye to wipe away a tear. For a fleeting moment he entertained the notion the heartfelt tears of a just man, might just wash the cataracts away, and God, in his great mercy, might heal him. He wiped his eyes, but still did not see. I am unclean, a sinner worse than all, he thought, and then he added the verbal period to his request. Taking a deep breath he added aloud: "Amen."

Robert Wanless

Chapter 5

In the city of Ecbatana, Sarah and the Demon, Asmodeaus, have a confrontation.

In the burgeoning country of Media, nearly three hundred miles to the southeast of Nineveh, was the city of Ecbatana. Ecbatana was situated high up in a rich fertile valley in the Zagros Mountains. In addition to its strong agricultural base, it was a major stopping point for caravans. It was an unusual city for many reasons, of which we will go into in some detail later on in our story.

Now, in this city, on the very same day which had seen the nadir of Tobit's life, another soul was rapidly plummeting to the depths of hers. She is Sarah, the beautiful daughter of Raguel, a fellow clansman and, indeed, also a kinsman to Tobit. Sarah is the only child of Raguel and his good wife, Edna, and had come late to them. They had cherished her as only older parents can cherish an only child, the only fruit of a deep and enduring love. She had been, as you would suppose, well cared for, perhaps even to the point of spoiling. Great care had been tendered on and to her, careful schooling in scripture and the traditions of her people, in the arts and in her own culture, and the rustic culture round about her. She was now in her twentieth year and considered a great beauty: tall, slender, gently curvaceous, and with a long dark, soft and shimmering fall of hair, carefully washed and scented. Her face was free of blemish or marks save for a hint of a dimple on either side of her sweet mouth. But foremost, she was gracious, courageous and wise. Her nimble fingers wove lovely melodies on her lyre as well as intricate patterns in embroidery. And her voice came close, or so neighbors and friends insisted, to rivaling that of an angel, whether she sang or spoke.

But, in spite of all this, in spite of the care and protection, the lavish provisions and gifts, in spite of the prayers and service given to and for her, she had been cursed with a curious and singular trial. This trial boggled the mind and weighed heavily on the heart of those closest to her, as well as the wisdom of physicians and advisors. She was suffering the effects, and consequential taunts, of a life seemingly gone awry -- not by her own doing, mind you, but by the machinations of a creature committed to making a mess of people's lives -- a Daemon named *Asmodeaus*. The heinous burden she had to live with was this: seven times she had been betrothed and on each of the seven wedding nights the bridegroom had died. The deaths had all appeared to be of "natural causes". While she had not been held responsible for them, she nevertheless had to bear the almost unthinkable burden of such a thing happening at all.

We join her then in the late morning of the very day mentioned earlier. Her maidservant has just pushed the young lady to her limits. The maid was a girl slightly younger than her mistress, a rather rough girl from one of the mountain tribes of Media. These girls were often hired for service in the well to do families. They were smart, strong, healthy, and curiously honorable -- which is to say they didn't steal. The girl's name was Kashima. While she was normally rather abrupt, even a little hard-edged, she was conscientious, hard working and given to the pleasant habit of whistling, much of the time, airs and tunes from the mountain shepherds and songs her tribe. Over the past month or so, she had not been whistling as much, and she had been growing increasingly surly towards Sarah, ever more abrupt, skirting the edge of rudeness. But not until today, had she actually provoked her mistress.

It happened like this: Sarah had taken to sleeping later and later, and then rising but staying in her room most of the morning, rarely coming out until sometime in the afternoon. Kashima, who also assisted Sarah's mother, must have felt the

Tobias and the Angel

young mistress was causing her more work than was bargained for. That coupled with the fact that the girl, like many, who assisted the well to do families, listened to the gossip at the market and the washing places.

Today, after her bath, Sarah sat at her dressing table as Kashima combed out her hair to set it into braids. Sarah was looking out her bedroom window, rather daydreaming, when the girl who had been scowling and avoiding looking at or talking to her mistress, suddenly and seemingly deliberately, pulled her hair.

The sharp pain caught Sarah unawares, and she overreacted, rebuking the maid sharply: "Ouch, Kashima! You careless, wretch! I wish you would try to be more careful! You aren't doing one of your family's goats!"

The girl looked at Sarah with a look that bordered on defiance, but said nothing. She continued combing Sarah's hair, but quickly, almost savagely, acting more and more in a frenzy.

Sarah looking at the girl in the mirror went on, "I believe you did that on purpose. Didn't you? I don't know what has become of you lately. But you are growing increasingly careless, rude and surly. I want it stopped."

Kashima did stop, and said, "God will that we never see a son or daughter of yours brought to light!"

"What? What are you talking about? And what a cruel thing to say! Mind your tongue, girl! I will not tolerate your insolence any longer. If you do not behave I will have my father dismiss you."

"Better that than your doing away with me."

"Do away with you? What are you talking about?"

"Everyone knows about it. I don't want to stay on with you anymore." Sarah looked at her incredulously, but slowly what the girl was talking about became clear; helped by: "Where are those husbands of yours?" The girl was easing backwards toward the door. "You've already been given in marriage to seven, and none of them has survived the wedding night with you. If you're one of those who wants no commerce with men, then why don't you just confess it to your parents and be done with it. Why have these young fellows come here full of hope and manly desire only so you can kill them?"

"What is this! Are you swallowing the vicious gossip of the market and the dung pile? Stop this now, or else!"

"Or else you will make as short work of me as you did the poor seven you sent on? I'm wondering if I be the your next target. Go. Join your husbands!" She spit out, and bolted from the room.

The maid had indeed been wallowing in one of the chief subjects of gossip in the entire city, which was no small town, by the way. It was, in fact, the new capital of Media, and as mentioned a major crossroads on several primary trade routes. So gossip didn't just stay in Ecbatana. Various versions of the unusual story had spread throughout the Hebrew communities in the Zagros, and had reached down to Nineveh and beyond.

What was not known, however, was that the deaths had been brought on not by any overt action on the part of the lovely Sarah, but rather by a jealous demon who had taken up his abode in the young lady's home. This creature bore a name in the old Median language which rendered into the Hebrew as *Asmodeaus*.

He was known in this area and among those to the south, as the demon of lust. His primary goal was the corruption of maidens, virgins in particular, by inflaming them with lust, as harmful in the marriage bed as out. Only a few of the native "Magi" suspected this, but they weren't kindly disposed to the Hebrews and their insistence on only "One God" so they kept it to themselves. But a demon is not a God, merely one of the unfortunately large number of fallen angels who spend their time going about causing mischief and misery.

Tobias and the Angel

Of course, the maid, Kashima, knew nothing of this and she was understandably nervous just being around her young mistress. She had reached the point where she didn't want to chance being alone with Sarah anymore. The maid's harsh words stung Sarah even though she wasn't ignorant of what was being said about her. She knew, too, that suspicions about her were increasingly, and more loudly, and brazenly, being whispered. It was only the position of her parents in the community, their reputation as being upright, courteous, and generous in alms giving, which quelled a serious response.

But even her mother and father, both of whom doted on the poor girl, had, of late, shown a tendency to be a little withdrawn from her. Their concerns went beyond the comparatively serious business of getting one's daughter married off, and well. It went beyond the sure knowledge that people were talking about them behind their back. It was the awareness, or suspicion, that perhaps, somehow, somewhere, something they had done displeased God, the Almighty, and so had brought on this tragic disfavor.

Now, the maid's taunt, hearing her worse fears blurted out this way, all added to the suffering Sarah was already enduring. While appearing poised, quiet, and seemingly aloof, Sarah had reached a breaking point. Alone now in her dressing room, and looking at her face in the mirror, which, try as she might to hide it, clearly showed the strain on her brow, she was unable to stifle a heart-breaking sob. She quickly, but quietly, retreated upstairs to the room she thought of as her "quiet place", where she went to be alone, to think or pray, in her father's house. But this room had become of late another place, a place where she hid and endured awful temptations and dreadful, shameful, thoughts. She was drawn there as some are to danger, to a precipice on a dare, to the brink of evil, to savor the superficial pleasures which can, if left unrestrained, accompany temptation; the fragrance as it were, of something, without the total soul-destroying imbibing.

She entered the room, and tried again to stifle the pain in her heart. She was able to do so and then she sat on the bed. It was a beautiful bed of carved wood, the finely carved wood, filigrees trimmed in gold leaf. The thick mattress was filled with the plucking of the Kapok tree from the Indus. It had been bought for her by her father to be her wedding bed. It had become the seeming, sad altar for the offerings of her seven "husbands." She pulled at the old cloth cover her mother had spread upon the bed to cover and protect it, and began tearing, feverishly, long strips from the cloth.

Things had indeed come to a head. Now the voice, which in the past had been more like her own, coming from the depth of her, summoning her to taste forbidden things, suddenly became quite audible. Even though it was bright and sunny outside, warm and balmy, inside the room it felt cold and damp, and there was a vile smell. There was no mistaking it; the voice was real, rather like a whistling or hissing sound, but still, a deep voice, a chilling voice, like none she had ever heard before. It spoke thus: "Ahhh. Poor dear. You are so sad. Now your maid is onto you."

The sound of it, at first, frightened her. But in a moment she mustered her courage and hissed back: "You Beast! At last you've made yourself known! Accursed one!"

The creature was manifest, as a chilling dark presence across the room. It was Asmodeaus, the demon, all right. He actually chuckled, rather as a series of quick coughs: "Good, my sweet, lamenting your sad virginity, like Lot's daughters, are you? And your lovely young body yearns for its fruition, now, doesn't it?"

"Horrid beast!" She spat out at him.

"Horrid beast!" He mimicked her perfectly. "You are young, beautiful, vibrant, and alive, how you crave satisfaction ...You are wet and beginning to breath deeply."

"I crave only your leaving me," she said, quickly, not wanting to consider the things he was saying.

"Your body has burned for your young men, seven times. Seven times I've deprived you. Come, now. Let us be united."

Sarah yelled a prayer, almost, up to heaven: "Oh God! Is there no rest from this vile beast?"

"Not a mere beast, my dearest one. No. I'm on a much higher plane than that."

Sarah stopped and forced herself to consider this. A higher plane? Admitting now that he existed; recognizing him as one apart from herself, Sarah was beginning to feel up to the battle. Maybe she needed to be more direct in her attack. Maybe she didn't have to be afraid -- or maybe she just didn't care anymore. Resignation can pass as courage, or is it the seed of courage. Anyway, Sarah went on to answer the beast's confession to being on a higher plane, "You couldn't prove it by me -- and further more, you smell."

"You love it, admit it. It is that earthy smell of someone consumed with desire. Men smell like this when they are about to enter..."

"For God's sake, shut up! Have you no decency at all."
"Well, hardly! But don't change the subject; come now; come and join me in a sweet ecstasy."

"I would join you in hell first." She began braiding the strips of cloth she had torn from the protecting coverlet.

"Ahhhh! But what is hell? Could such a pleasure be in a place like you think of as Hell? Come, now. Let us be united; A carrot, a cucumber, even your fingers; and you will have me -- and I will have you.

"I'd die first!"
"Yes, that's it! The ultimate ecstasy -- Death by lust!
"You disgust me!"
"You love it."
"Will you go away!"

"Leave you? No, my dear, my place is with you, I won't go. And none in this land have the power to rid you of me. Lay back on the bed now, and come with me."

"I've more of you now than I can bear!"

"You like it when I talk to you like that, don't you. Come now, Ah, what an eternity we'll share, you and I ..."

"Yucch! You're right. What an eternity! Oh to be rid of you!" Sarah got up off the bed. She had been braiding the cloth until now she had the beginnings of a rope. She walked first to the window, then back. Then looking up she began to consider the center beam of the roof. She thought of adding the tie of her robe to the braided rope, tying them together. Then she could get up on a chair and tie it to the beam, then around her neck, and kicking the chair out from under her she could hang herself."

The demon guessed her thoughts: "I've heard it said that the ultimate satisfaction can come at the moment one hangs herself. Men even experience an erection, sometimes-even ejaculate when they're hung. It's that ultimate ecstasy. Do it!"

Sarah stopped and looked in the direction of the beast. "Ah, now I see what you're about. I kill myself then others will just reproach my father and say to him, "You had one dear daughter and she hanged herself because of her troubles." Then he loses his spirit through grief and you, or one of your minions gets him ... You bag two for one!"

"Oh, how can you say such things?"

Sarah began to feel she might have him on the run: "My death will bring my aged father in sorrow to his grave. No, I will not hang myself; it would be better to beg the Lord God to let me die and not live on to hear your vile prompting and that silly girl's reproaches. Then you lose this round."

"Hsssss!" Said the daemon.

"What a fitting sound, you slimy snake!" Sarah, with new resolve, not in desperation, not even in anger, fell to her knees,

Tobias and the Angel

and with all the spiritual energy she could muster, she prayed, "Oh, my dear God! I've had enough of this beast, these lies, this life!"

"It won't do you any good, Sweetheart; God doesn't hear your prayers anymore. He's abandoned you -- and all your countrymen. Why do you think you are here? It was all that Jeroboam's fault, wasn't it? ... Those Golden Calves -- and they were so tacky! And he knows that you secretly want me ..."

"Oh God! Please!"

"Please, please, please me. You're wasting your time. He's not listening."

And Sarah spread out her hands in prayer and with tears falling across her lovely cheek, she begged God to free her from her sorrows, as all the while the demon tried to drown her prayers with his hissing, whistling and noises. But still Sarah continued to pray:

Blessed is thy name, O God of our fathers,
Who, though thy anger be roused, shows mercy,
Who pardons the sinner who cries out to thee in time of need!
To thee, Lord, I now turn.
Lord, my prayer is that thou would either rid me of these
clogging suspicions, and this vile gnawing beast,
or take me to thyself.
Thou, Lord, know well I have never lusted after a man;
that I have guarded my soul from shameful desire,
avoided the wanton, and cast not my lot with the dalliant.
When I consented to take a Husband,
O Lord, it was thy law, not my lust, that was my rule.
Perhaps I was unworthy of these men,
or they of me;
or maybe thou were reserving me for yet another --
thy designs are beyond our human reach.
But this at least all thy true worshippers know;

Robert Wanless

> *never was a life of trials but had its crown;*
> *never distress from which thou couldst not save;*
> *never a punishment but left a gateway to thy mercy;*
> *the storm passes, and thou grantest clear weather again;*
> *crying ceases and thou fillest the cup with rejoicing.*
> *But, whatever, I say to thee, blessed be thy name,*
> *O God of Israel, forever!"*

The young woman's face became radiant, and tears of joy flowed down her softly downed cheeks. She sobbed for just a moment, and with her finely shaped jaw set, firm and handsome, she raised her lovely face to heaven and all but shouted: "AMEN!"

"I'll be back," The demon hissed, and was gone in a sharp, chilled, smelly breeze.

* * *

And so it was that at that moment, the prayers of both these poor souls, Sarah and Tobit, ascended to heaven and found their way, as all good prayers must, into the glorious presence of Almighty God, He Who Is. And this kind and loving God, who yearns to be thought of and loved as a father, had mercy on them both, poor Tobit, and dear Sarah. And he set in motion his kindness. He summoned into his glorious presence no less a personage than the great archangel, Raphael, one of his seven holy archangels, he who's name means "God has Healed" and sent him, in person, to go out and bring deliverance to these two suppliants of that moment.

Chapter 6

Tobias is sent on an errand, and hires a guide

Tobit awoke the next morning from a deep, sound, sleep following that tearful, faith-filled, heartfelt, and as it turned out, fateful prayer. He awoke feeling rested and very much at peace, in fact feeling positively happy. He was almost sorry he had prayed to die. But he accepted his newfound peace of mind rather as a confirmation that his request for death had been granted.

He arose from his bed and dressed. He slipped into a tunic, then his sandals, thinking as he did so that he had become adept at many things he had once taken for granted, then had to relearn to perform them. Now he was almost taking them for granted again.

Before standing up, he remembered the dream he had had, or it seemed like a dream at the time, anyway. It had come just before waking. Awake now, and recalling it, it seemed more real than a dream. Someone had called to him in this dream, and reminded him about the money he had invested with his cousin Gabelus' import/export business, ten, maybe fifteen years ago. Gabelus live in the city of Reges, way down in lower Media. The someone, or something who had called to him was some ethereal kind of being, more like a light, with a voice. Maybe it was an angel, he thought. Anyway, that had been what mentioned the money to him.

"Of course!" he said, aloud. "How could I have forgotten that?" He stood up, feeling at once excited, relieved, and even more at peace. He felt his way to the chest at the foot of the bed. In the chest he felt around for a piece of parchment, about the size of his hand. Flat on the bottom of the upper tray he felt it. With a sigh and a smile, he slipped it into his tunic. The money would provide for Anna and Tobias when he had passed on. "Yes," he thought, "his prayer had been answered."

Before starting down the steps he rapped on Tobias' door and called to him, "Tobias, son, come join me."

The boy, ever obedient, was down the steps almost before the older man was off them. "Come with me into the courtyard, Son, and break some bread with me."

Rebeccah, the girl, was already up and took Tobit's arm, gently escorting him outside. She helped him onto the bench and went back to the kitchen and returned carrying a tray with bowls of cereal made of cracked wheat berries, toasted in the oven served in goats' milk and flavored with raisins, almonds and honey. Tobias followed, joining his father. She handed the older man one of the bowls, and placed Tobias' across from him, avoiding his eyes, as she placed the bowl on a small table. Rebeccah would not look directly at the young man. She always blushed and got flustered when she did so. Next she returned with hot tea.

The two men sat together on the bench beneath the fig tree. After a brief prayer of thanksgiving, they began quietly eating their breakfast. The morning was still and cool, with the chirping of sparrows, the complaints of an old jay, and songs of other birds filling the air. They listened awhile to Old Joseph puttering in his shed, and Rebeccah working in the kitchen.

After eating together quietly for a few minutes, Tobit spoke: "Son, when God takes my soul to himself, I fear we won't be in our homeland. I want you to give this body of mine burial in the field there beyond our house. Then I want thee to give thy mother (The use of the formal pronoun alerted the boy to the seriousness of what his father was saying. Formality was unusual in their relationship). I want thee to give thy mother her due -- while her life lasts. Do not forget the hazard she underwent to bear thee in her womb."

Tobias and the Angel

The boy nodded acknowledgement, but showed concern over his father's words and the subject matter.

Tobit took a piece of the warm bread Rebeccah had brought out, dipped it in the milk and chewed it quietly. Tobit went on, "When she too has lived out her allotted span of years, bury her at my side." The gentleman's voice began to assume the prayerful quality it did when he recited the psalms,

And while thou hast life, think ever upon God,
Avoid all sinful designs, and
Keep the commandments of the Lord our God fulfilled.
Use thy wealth in giving of alms;
Never turn thy back on any man who is in need,
And the Lord, in thy own need, will bless thee.
Show to others what kindness thy means allow,
Giving much, if much is thine, if thou hast little,
Cheerfully sharing that little.
Share thy bread with the hungry and the poor,
In thy garments let the naked go clad.
To do this is but to lay up a store against
The day of distress.
The giving of alms covers a multitude of sins.
Also, keep clear of loose women,
Save thyself for thy wife.
In thought and word, pride must never rule;
Through it all, our undoing came.
Pay thy workman his wages;
Do not let the money he has earned
Remain in thy keeping.
Take a wise man's counsel over thy doings;
But ask God to guide thy paths aright.
Let all thy designs repose in Him.
Never lose heart, my son,
Though we lead the life of the poor men,
If we but keep close to God,

Robert Wanless

> *And do the good we can,*
> *Blessings shall be ours in abundance.*
> *Amen.*

"Amen," the lad said, almost in a reflex action, then quickly added, "But Father..."

"Please, Son. Let me continue while all I must say is in my mind. Now then, when you were little, I invested some money, ten talents of silver, with a fellow clansman of ours in the city of Rages, in Media. He is a distant uncle or cousin, I suppose, anyway, we are linked by blood, from my mother's side, I think. His name is Gabelus. I still have his bond. I want you to go to his home in Rages and present him with the bond. He has prospered well in the business so there should be no difficulty in his returning the money, and with a handsome interest."

Tobias looked at his father incredulously. "Father, why have you waited till now?"

"Son, I forgot. This has been a long and difficult period in our life. With so much else it very simply slipped my mind."

"Well, of course, I will do all that you have told me, Father. But, what is all this talk about burying you? You have many years yet to live. Your health is good."

"Please. I know that my time is short."

"Father, how can I do anything with a heart heavy at the thought of losing you?"

"It is part of becoming a man, Son. I lost my own dear father when I was but a boy. I don't remember ever seeing him."

"Well, be that as it may. Maybe when I get this money we can seek out a competent physician to heal you?"

"A competent one! I've lost one fortune to that bunch; you want I should lose another?"

"Well, we'll see. How shall I get this money from our relative? He doesn't know me and I do not know him. What proof shall I give to make him believe me, that the bond I present is true, so he will give me the money?"

"Gabelus is a fellow countryman, and clansman; he is an honest man. I have continued to buy from him over the years. He gave me the note with his hand mark, and I gave him mine. These we cut in half. He pulled the two pieces of parchment from the belt of his tunic. You show him the two halves. He matches them with the two that he has, that's it. It's been many years since I made this investment so it should be worth a great deal now. Now the bond you will find written on papyrus in a small box hidden under the floorboards in your mother's and my room, near the door to the landing."

They were quiet again. Tobias thought about all his father had said. There was, he had to admit, inherent in his father's words, a call to adventure in going to distant Rages. But he felt it wouldn't look right to seem excited. He said, "I don't know the roads in Media, or how to get there. Furthermore, Father, I don't believe they are under Assyrian control anymore. This could be very dangerous." He was having difficulty suppressing his excitement.

"Humm," the older man sighed. He thought, "The boy is a cautious one. Maybe officers' school might help." He went on, "If you go to the Great Caravansary, the one near the Assur Road Gate, most days there are caravans arriving there from the mountains, from Reges by Ecbatana, and from the south, Ur, from where our ancestor, Abraham came. There are usually guides looking for a caravan to ride with or for work. You want someone who seems reliable to go with you. Find someone of our own people. We will get him to agree to payment on your return, your safe return, and with all the money from Gabelus.

"What about mother?" Tobias asked.

"We are doing this for your mother, and for you, of course."

* * *

Tobias walked out of the house and stepped into the fresh, warm, morning air. The prospect of the journey before him lightened his step. He walked from the house to the Great Bazaar Road, then on downtown. At the great Bazaar he turned left onto Palace Street, the great promenade which stretched from north to south, the length of the city. He looked ahead, down the grand wide boulevard, feeling his excitement increase. The boulevard was, as always, busy with traffic; chariots rushing to and fro, crowds of people, street vendors, small intercity caravans, squads of soldiers marching in formation, elegantly dressed bureaucrats, workers of every sort, messengers and delivery men with hand carts. He walked while looking side to side at the magnificent city all about him. He passed the small but ornate tomb of the Prophet Jonah, the prophet who had come to Nineveh some seventy years ago to warn the city of impending doom. Jonah's warning had saved the city, and the cranky old man had stayed on in Nineveh an honored citizen, and more so by the Ninevites than by his own people, the Hebrews. Tobias felt a certain affection for the grouchy old Prophet. While Jonah was a fellow Israeli, Tobias couldn't but feel thankful that the man had saved Nineveh. While he hoped to see again the land of his birth, Nineveh was the only home he had ever known.

The excitement of the city fed the excitement building within him. "I will go to Rages and I will get the money. I will help; I will save my father!" went through his mind, over and over as he walked along, walking faster and faster, heading to The Great Caravansary at the southern end of the city. From nearly a half mile away he could see the roof of the Great Caravansary, high up above all the others in the largely industrial area. Getting closer still, he could see the activity leading to and coming from it, he could soon hear the place, and then he could smell it.

Tobias and the Angel

The caravans came here mainly from out of the south and the southeast, from the Indus, Persia, Media, and Susa and even Babylonia. They came from the forests and mines of the Zagros and from the marshes to the south. But they came also from the north, the Armenian areas, Urahtu, Lake Urnia. Here stopped mainly those caravans terminating in Nineveh. Caravans continuing on to Anatolia, and the west, often went round the city walls north to the smaller, but still very busy caravansary by the Anatolian Road Gate.

Just approaching the place, his heart was beating faster. After his father had bought the stand, he had come here a few times with his father to help him carry items back. Then he had only been in the great yard outside the building, where vendors set up stands. But coming here with his father was one thing; approaching it now, alone, Tobias began to feel, really for the first time, he had become a man. Now he was doing something for someone else, giving back to those from whom he had always received. He knew that what he was doing for his father and mother was something important which only he could do.

He stopped for a moment to look with awe at the huge building. It sat in the middle of a vast area of several acres, two sides of which were formed by the south and west walls of the city. The building was larger than the king's palace. It was as big in area as Sargon's temple at Dur Sharrukin, not as magnificent of course, nor as colorful, but vastly more important and exciting. In fact he had heard it said that the Caravansary was one of the wonders of Nineveh. The side which opened onto the boulevard, showed one of the two main entrances, the one which was the more ornate. Four columns graced either side of the opening. These columns were topped with bird like creatures. Between them were large, long, capping stones on which was carved "The God Assur Protects Nineveh." On either side of the building, balconies jutted out and these were protected by the overhang of the massive tiled roof.

He stopped for a moment and put his hand to his neck to hide a deep swallow as he looked up at the building again. He had no idea where he would have to go to find a guide. He would just find his way around inside. He didn't want to seem stupid, or young, so he headed right to the building, trying to act as though he actually came here two or three times a week, acting very much like he knew what he was doing.

He walked through the large entrance into the building and stepped into what felt like a physical presence. The presence was made up of light, smell, sounds, and more. This presence was so strong that he paused momentarily, and involuntarily. He paused also for his eyes to adjust to the light inside. Bright light poured down onto the floor of the building from the massive "skylights" high above, and from the two large entrances at either end of the building as well as from numerous other entrances and large windows. Dust and hundreds of items reflected and diffused the light to such a degree everyone had to develop special vision inside.

The main floor was as big as a polo field. The center of the floor where the animals were loaded and unloaded was gravel and sand. The perimeter, where the massive tables and racks on which the loads from the caravans were removed for sorting, distributing, rerouting and selling, was paved with large flagstones. It was around this area that much, but not all, the amazing activity of the caravansary took place; and all of it in this peculiar hazy light.

In addition to the light making up the curious presence, there was the smell: an incense made up of manure and urine from what could be up to a thousand animals. There were also the smells of at least as many people. There was the fragrance of commodities brought into the building from all over the world.

Then there were the sounds: the noises of hundreds upon hundreds of animals; horses, camels, donkeys, asses, cattle, goats, to name only the more common. Then, adding to their braying, honking, squawking, and the clicking of hundreds of hooves on flagstones, there was the sound of caravan masters, and skinners. This was inside the building. Outside there was added to this the cries of hawkers peddling unclaimed freight, myriad products and produce; hundreds of people speaking in a cacophonous polyglot; the cries of workers, or men or boys, seeking work, for a day or even a few hours, and women seeking buyers for their wares; add to this the tones and pitches of hundreds of bells on animals, and other racket beyond description; and all the colors of the world, the products of the world, the people of the world; it surpassed anything, for those who could take it. If one hadn't the stomach for it, however, it could all be overwhelming, and it usually was. Tobias stepped into it then, and was forced to catch his breath, an act which he quickly realized ran the risk of causing one to gag.

The first caravans of the season, the ones in the early spring, and the last ones in the late fall, sometimes numbered several hundred animals and personnel, one of these caravans could fill the caravansary. The rest of the time several caravans could be served at once. Today was a busier day than usual, although, to those not used to the place, even a comparatively quiet day was a very busy day.

Tobias' attention was arrested by what he saw in the center of the floor. Two caravans, one of at least three dozen donkeys had just arrived with fur from up near Lake Yanuk, in Northern Media, just as another caravan much larger was leaving for the Indus region, loaded with various items from Nineveh. Commands from the masters of the two caravans were being shouted and were in conflict with each other. These were confusing the skinners and the beasts. Tempers were thin and beginning to flare in the morning heat. The commands soon turned into shouting and cursing matches, then came teasing from the onlookers, the braying and honking of the animals, all accompanied by the background music of the animals' bells.

The two caravan masters rushed at each other and squared off, the one carrying a scimitar, the other a club.

Suddenly a short, broad shouldered, dark man, wearing a saffron colored turban and short britches, charged into the forming melee carrying a long pole. He began shouting commands and insults at the two caravan masters who both, immediately, got themselves, skinners and animals under control. He was the floor master, used to trouble, and more than able to stop it. In a moment, a semblance of peace was restored, with laughter from the onlookers, but a mild disappointment at missing what had briefly promised to be a good, but bloody fight. With a cheerful wave from the master of the departing caravan, and a resentful one from the arriving, the main floor returned to a semblance of order.

Tobias had begun looking around for someone who looked like he might be a guide. But what did a guide look like, he wondered. He saw a man, whom he vaguely recognized from buying expeditions with his father, and walked over to ask him if he knew of, or could recommend, a guide. Tobias strained to hear above the din what the man was saying. The man finally pointed over to the Floor Master, the saffron-turbaned fellow who had calmed the dispute. He was now heading up to the platform from which he kept watch of the floor. Tobias sprinted over and started up the stairs behind him trying to get to him before he resumed his duties. He was stopped. A gruff looking man with a foul breath said: "Can't go up -- Floor Masters only." "I want to talk to that fellow," Tobias yelled up to the floor master: "Sir, I'm Tobias ben Tobit. I think you know my father. I'm looking for a guide to take me to Rages, in Media!"

The man stopped and looked at Tobias, shrugged his shoulders and said:"Plenty around. Help yourself."

"How? Where? What do they look like?"

The man rubbed his chin and smiling, said: "Well," and people nearby stopped and listened, waiting for what the floor

Tobias and the Angel

master was going to say: "if you see someone who looks smart, well-dressed for the road, seems to know what he's doing... forget him. That will be one of the donkeys."

This was followed with laughter and some derisive comments from the crowd and this comment from one: "Yeah, if it's a real ugly one, it's his wife!"

"And if it's pregnant and doesn't know the sire, it's your daughter!" The floor master fired back, without missing a beat.

He went on talking to Tobias, "The best thing is to hang around the canteen over there. One or two always turn up there. You might even find a sober one – it's still early."

Tobias nodded his thanks and started across the floor toward the canteen. The "Canteen" was the back wall of the building, distinguished from the rest of the building with a sign and two large barrels of beer on racks against the wall behind a long counter. By the counter there were tubs of a tea like beverage, for those looking for a jump without the buzz. He could see only the backs of men standing at, or leaning against, the counter. He noticed it wasn't as if anyone wore a sign saying, "Guide for Hire." He saw some men whom he thought might be guides, but also looked tough, more like the kind from whom you hire protection.

One particular man caught Tobias' attention. He seemed particularly dirty, and had large dark arms sticking out of a leather mantle, these were covered with tattoos, and he could see, as he got closer, the man also had a tattoo on his forehead. Tobias fortified himself to begin asking each of the men in turn if he were a guide. Then something latching onto his ankle stopped him.

He looked down to see a dog, a medium sized, rather good looking canine, a golden haired wolf-like creature, acting like he was about to clamp his jaws on Tobias' ankle. "Hey, dog, watch out!" Tobias said and kicked his leg out, not to hit but to discourage the animal. He looked back up to find himself almost blinded by the appearance of a tall, handsome, man. Tobit blinked his eyes, then averted them, as one does when suddenly blinded by the sun reflected of a glass or shiny metal object.

He looked back and was able to see a young man, in his late twenties or early thirties. His hair was wheat colored, like his dog's, and wavy, trimmed neatly and curled under at his shoulders. He was, although bright, intelligent, and clean looking, not a like a dandy. Such a fellow would not be here. And he had about him a strong, solid, look of a man who knows what's to be done, and he was the one to do it. His face was smooth, clean-shaven, with a handsome brow, a manly jaw, a sly smile on his lips, and a delightful twinkle in his eye.

The man was dressed in a well-tailored and remarkably clean white tunic. It was cut, Judean style, just below the knees, trimmed with silver bric-a-brac, and with a maroon colored mantle over it.

He said to Tobias: "There, now, see how the good Lord provides? The pooch was just looking for a nice bone to gnaw on, and there is your ankle."

"Perhaps, Sir, you don't feed your dog properly. In any case, I would certainly appreciate his not making my ankle his lunch."

"He won't eat much. And by the looks of you, it's just as well."

Looking down at his legs Tobias said, "I admit they aren't that thick, mostly bone, but they're all I've got to connect my foot bones to my leg bones."

"Catchy little phrase, there. You write poetry?" The man clapped his hands twice and said, "Stop that Nimrod!"

"Not really. But I am studying to be a scribe."

"Is that why you're here at the Caravansary?"

"No. Right now, I'm here looking for a guide to take me to Rages. Do you know of any?"

Tobias and the Angel

"As a matter of fact I do -- intimately," and he pointed to himself using both his thumbs.

"You're a guide? You don't look like a guide."

"Ahh. What does a guide look like? As a matter of fact, yes, I am -- yes. I guess I don't look the part. It's these togs. The tailor, from whom I bought them in Damascus, assured me this is what all the well-dressed guides are wearing this season. Actually, I rather thought I looked like an Assyrian Prince. I fooled you. Of course, in the scale of worth, guides are of far greater value than princes, anyway. Judging by the princes I've seen they can't be worth much. That Damascus tailor! You can't trust a foreigner."

"Well, if you bought the togs in Damascus, was it not you that were the foreigner?"

"You are wise for one so young. True enough, I was the foreigner. Still am, for that matter. I am an Israelite in this land of the Assyrian. One of your fellow countrymen, I believe; and I have come here to find work as a guide."

Tobias stood looking at the man's handsome, open, face, until the dog began growling and snapping at his ankle again. "The dog, Sir, he still has designs on my leg."

"He doesn't bite. At least he doesn't usually bite. Must be those tasty ankles of yours." He clapped his hands again and said, "Stop that Nimrod!"

"And, you are a guide for hire? What an amazing coincidence. Do you, by chance, know the road to Reges, in Media?"

"Ah ha, still another coincidence. I know it like the back of my hand. I not only know the way, I was hoping to land a job to get me there. Not a major job, mind you, just something to cover the expenses."

"Oh, too bad. I have to come back here as well."

"Why anyone would want to come back here is beyond me. So big, noisy, crowded."

65

"I don't mean here, this place. I mean Nineveh -- the city."

"Oh. Well, as cities go it seems a nice place to visit, but I sure wouldn't want to live here."

"I too would rather be in my homeland -- at least I think I would. We, that is, my family and I, are exiles. I was only a baby when I was brought here, but I've been here so long that I suppose now it's like home. I'm going to Rages now on an errand for my father. I will have to return."

"Well, actually, I have to come back here too. I'm on a special mission."

"This is really incredible! And you know the way there?"

"I've been there many times. I am familiar with all the different routes and know them all well. It is a full two days journey to Ecbatana and another two from there to Rages."

"Only two full days! Surely it's farther than that! Are you sure you've been there?"

"Well, maybe it does take a bit longer than two days. Traveling alone I often make much better time. But I know the way and I know the area. In my travels to Media I often lodge with one Gabelus, a fellow countryman of ours, who lives in Reges."

With one amazing coincidence after another Tobias just took this more or less in stride: "This is Incredible! You know where Gabelus lives! Wow! It is as though the Almighty has answered my prayer directly. It would be wonderful if you were to go with me. But, we do have one little problem, probably not even worth mentioning."

"Try it."

"I will pay you your wages, but, I can't do it until we return?"

"Humm. It's always something. I thought as much. Well, all right, you have an honest face, not terribly bright one, but an honest one."

Tobias and the Angel

"Can you wait here for me? I have to go home and talk to my father. I'll be right back."

"I'll wait, only don't be too long."

"Yes, I mean -- No, I won't. I mean, well ...I don't know why you can't come with me."

"I wondered the same thing."

The Guide indicated a side exit near the canteen and the two men left the presence of the Caravansary for Tobias' home -- followed by the dog. Along the way, Tobias plied the man with questions. The guide answered them and talked generally about the trip, the type of people one would meet along the way, and the bandits and the wild animals that were known to attack and kill travelers.

* * *

Tobias bounded through the front door and into the room where his father sat quietly meditating.

"Father, I have had the most extraordinary good fortune. I have found a fellow Israelite to accompany me to Reges. He says he both knows the way and he even knows the home of Gabelus, and he has even agreed to accept payment when we return."

The good news was almost too much for the older man. He looked toward his son, seeing only an indistinct form in a gray field. Tears, nevertheless, rolled down his cheek and into his beard. "This is extraordinary," he said. Then paused and frowned, "but we must always be cautious. Call the man in, son; let us find out about his family and tribe and make sure that he will be a trustworthy companion for you.

Tobias stuck his head out the front door and whispered to his companion: "Come in, sir, my father wants to meet you."

Robert Wanless

The man joined father and son in the darkened room, and grabbing the older man's two hands into his own, with his rich voice proclaimed: "I pray that all is well with you, good sir!"

Tobit looked toward his son: "What's this? I send you to hire a guide and you come back with an unemployed jester?" Then, to the man: "How I wish something could at last be well with me! How can anything be well with me --I am a blind man; I can see only shadows and gray. I hear men's voices, but the men I do not see. I cannot see the face of my dear wife -- who only ignores me. I cannot work; I've spent all my money on physicians. Though still alive, I am as good as dead. Now my only ..."

"Take heart, good man, in God's design. Your cure is at hand. Take heart."

"Humh! I was wrong, son. He's not a jester; he's another physician. You're wasting your time. I've no money!"

"Please, my good man. Will you stop your worrying? I'm not here for money. True enough, I am something of a healer, but not, strictly speaking a physician. Right now I'm working as a guide."

"That's more like it. My son, Tobias here, wishes to travel to Rages in Media to collect a bond owed me by one Gabelus. If you can go with him as his guide I will pay you. Of course, we are not able to do so at this point in time."

"There are no points in time. But, yes. I can go with him. I go often to Media. I have traveled over all the plains and mountains there and I am familiar with all its roads."

Tobit cursed his blindness, thinking: The face of this man I want to see. Is all this possible? Is the man a charlatan, or a confidence man, with mischief on his mind?'

"Where is your trust, my friend?"

"And you are an Israelite?" Tobit asked.

"That I am, good Tobit."

Tobias and the Angel

"This is truly remarkable. Then, tell me, my friend, what family and tribe you belong to."

"Why do you need to know my tribe?"

"I do not need to know, my friend, I only wish to know whose son you are, and what your name is."

"Ahhh. Yes, of course." The fellow looked at Tobit, smiled and said, "I am called Azarias, son of the older Ananias, of your tribe of Naphtali, a kinsman."

"Azarias. Hmmm. Azarias ben Ananias!" It seemed right, thought Tobit, but it had been well over twenty years, and the fellow's voice, like his very presence inspired confidence. "Forgive me for doubting thy lineage;" again, Tobias noted the formal pronouns. "Thou comest of good stock indeed. Now, don't be angry with me, my friend, because I wished to know the facts of thy descent. Thou are a kinsman, and a man of good family. I knew Ananias and Nathan the two sons of the older Semelias. They used to go with me to Jerusalem and worship with me there; they never went astray. Thy kinsmen are worthy men; thou come of a sound stock, indeed ... even though I don't recall having met thee, or of Ananias mentioning thee."

Tobias, as enthusiastic about his guide as he was, couldn't help but detect a certain hesitancy in the way Azarias had answered his father. He couldn't help noting too, that as he talked he kept his hands behind his back.

Tobit went on, "I will pay you a drachma a day and allow you the same expenses as my son. I ask only that you keep him company on his travels, keep him from harm, and deliver him safely to Gabelus and back to me. Do so in good time and I will add something to your wages."

"Have no fear. I will go with him, and we shall travel there and back without mishap, because with me the road is safe, or at least fairly safe."

"Tobias, my boy, get ready what you need for the journey. The box I spoke of in my room, go to it and bring the bond; and there are several coins wrapped in a silk cloth in the box, bring them; bring the whole box, to me. And you, Azarias, you have a donkey, or mule?

"I can rent the use of one. I normally don't use a beast in my travels."

"You'll need provisions for two? Some tea, meal, fruit of course... I'll have Rebeccah prepare some things."

"The boy can fish along the way. And in the mountains game abounds."

"Yes, so I've heard. Just make sure that you yourselves do not become prey."

Rebeccah had been standing outside the room listening and adoring Tobias as she usually did from a distance. She went to the kitchen to put together the provisions for the trip. Tobit called Old Joseph in and told him to help prepare for the trip. Tobias was told to get "a bedroll, a spare tunic, another pair of sandals, the like. Where is your mother?"

Rebeccah, preparing items in the kitchen, signaled to Anna who had been listening quietly from the workroom in the back, to the goings on in the front room. She came out and watched as her only son came down the steps. His face was flushed with the excitement of the impending trip. Anna began to feel an aching in her heart. She wanted to say something to her husband. But they had not talked since the terrible day of the accusation. She wanted to delay forgiving him for just another week, to extract sufficient guilt to balance the hurt she had felt. She wanted to say something, to question sending her son away on this trip. But there was in her husband's manner, a resolution, a conviction, in the way he looked and spoke, that inhibited her saying anything.

Tobit suggested the name of the man who ran one of the caravan services as someone who might provide a reliable animal for the journey. The three men talked together, reviewing the things they would need, where they were going,

Tobias and the Angel

checking again the bonds, which had been stored under the floor. Tobit was now satisfied they were ready. Rebeccah handed the provisions to Old Joseph, who in turn passed them on to Tobias. The old man had tears in his eyes as he handed the boy the items.

Tobit hugged his son and said, "Set off now with your kinsman, Son. May God in heaven keep both of you safe on your way there and restore you to me unharmed. And may his holy angel safely escort you both.

"Oh, he will. Have no fear," the smiling Azarias assured Tobit.

Tobias kissed his mother and father good bye, gave young Rebeccah a playful knuckle on her veil-covered head, he shook hands with old Joseph, promising to see him again soon, and telling him to take good care of his father. The two men stepped outside into the noonday light and heat, and together they set out on their way, with Tobias carrying most of the goods on his shoulder.

Poor Anna watched with tight jaws as the pair walked down the street, finally she could contain herself no longer; bursting into tears she broke her silence and finally spoke to her husband: "Why have you sent my boy away? Is he not our prop and stay? Has he not always been at home with us? Why send money after money? Why didn't you just write off that loan for the sake of our boy and let us be content to live the life the Lord has appointed for us.

Tobit didn't look in her direction, only straight ahead. "So, you've found your voice again? Don't worry; our son will go safely and come back safely. Don't worry or be anxious about him, my dear. I really believe that God will send a good angel with him and his journey will prosper, and he will come back safe and sound. You will live to see him with your own eyes on that day of his safe return."

"Hummph!" Anna said, and went back to her work, quietly sobbing.

Chapter 7
On the Road

The first stop on the trip to Rages was the caravansary to rent a donkey. Tobias carrying most of the equipment, in his excitement, all but ran ahead of Azarias and scarcely noticed the load he was carrying. Tobit had given his son what was surely the last bit of cash he had, a total of about ten shekels. Not a paltry sum, but about the lower limit of what it should take to get to Rages. Tobit had also recommended a certain man, a Jurzaeel, a nominal Israelite, but wise and fair, and a member of a consortium which owned several, and financed other, caravans. He had an office at the caravansary and would be able to provide them with, or information about, getting a donkey or camel to use on the trip.

When they arrived back at the caravansary, they went right to one of the sets of stairs leading to the second floor of the building. The second floor was rather more like a mezzanine and reached by the balcony, which surrounded three sides of the building. The mezzanine was a series of rooms, constructed of wood and built on the thick block walls of the building. These rooms were the offices for the caravansary bookkeepers, distributors, and fee collectors. That consortium, which owned, organized, or financed, caravans rented offices there too. There were also dormitories for caravan people, and individual rooms for the masters, and guest rooms for those who traveled with the caravans. The offices of the VIPs, or "principals," had large windows which opened onto the main floor to oversee the myriad activities below. Of course, they also permitted the heat, noise and smell to come in.

Tobias and Azarias entered one of the small, crowded, dirty offices, to which they had been directed. Tobias introduced himself to Jurzaeel, and told him obliquely about the nature of their journey, speaking vaguely about retrieving some of his father's property. The man was courteous, respectful, said he knew Tobit, asked about him, all the while looking the two over carefully. Azarias he found somewhat impressive and a competent looking guide. Jurzaeel agreed to rent them a donkey and took them down to the yard and the animal pens. He led them to a large corral of donkeys, which belonged to his group. He told a dark lazy-looking boy to single out a specific animal, which the boy did, throwing a bridle on it, and dragging the reluctant, sleepy-eyed creature over to them.

"He sure seems slow and reluctant," Tobias said.

"Donkeys" said the man with a shrug, indicating they were all that way.

Azarias carefully checked over the beast: "You're sure this old fellow will make it there and back?" he asked, skeptically.

"No doubt about it," the man said, patting the dusty flank of the creature, "and there's no mischievous spirit in him to trouble you along the way."

"Doesn't appear to be much spirit in him of any kind," Azarias said with a wink to Tobias, and a dubious expression to the owner.

"You really think the old boy will make it?" Tobias added.

"Stake my life on it."

"Hmmmmm," said Tobias.

"I usually take the Smugglers Road," Azarias said looking at the donkey, walking around him in a knowing way. "Will he be able to make the grades?"

"Why would you want to go that way? The new Little Zab route is safer, smoother, much more level, a better way."

"But at least a day longer, and not necessarily under Assyrian control. I'm not sure he'll make it?" Azarias insisted.

"Not make it? Ha! He's made it many times; could make it blindfolded. That's why it's so important for me to get him back. One of my best leads."

"If he's so good, why isn't he on the road now?" asked Azarias.

"Just a little rest up. I like to spell my animals. Six weeks on, one week off, as our" -- and here his voice dropped to a barely audible whisper -- "Lord, the Almighty -- his name be praised for ever ..."

'But very quietly..." Azarias added, completing the sentence in a teasing whisper.

"To be sure, to be sure..." Jurzaeel nodded, looking left and right, then drawing his finger across his throat, then added, "As He, decreed for all of us."

"That was six *days* of labor and one *day* of rest," Azarias corrected.

"I take the liberty of adjusting the time periods to compensate for our four legged servants' inability to keep time."

The conversation between the three drew several of the curious regulars of the caravansary, to gather around. Before long there was a small crowd, and they were profligate with offers of conflicting advice about the best routes, bandits of which to be careful, inns to be recommended.

When, with a shrug of resignation from Azarias, Tobias agreed on the donkey, Jurzaeel asked for a security deposit of five silver shekels.

"That is all the money we have for the journey, Jurzaeel. Surely you know my father is good for this."

"Your esteemed father, may The Almighty preserve and heal him, is presently of limited means, lad."

"That is the reason for the journey, Jurzaeel, to expand these limits," Azarias said with a knowing wink to the man.

With a shrug of helplessness he returned: "I've my investors to answer to..."

"If those investors trusted you, Jurzy, you sure as hell can trust this pair," came the good word from a wholesaler, from whom Tobit often bought, and who like the others had joined the gathering, adding his wisdom. Presently, at least four others assured Jurzaeel of Tobit's devotion, honesty, and reputation for success. This all finally served as an acceptable guarantee for the safe return of the aged beast, and with only a small deposit of a one shekel, "merely a token to pacify my investors" and with full payment for the rental assured on their return, agreement was reached.

While the financiers and advisors were discussing the rental, Tobias kept note how the donkey looked at Azarias with touching devotion, and moved close to him. With the deal consummated, they set about loading provisions onto the poor beast's back, and into the saddlebags that were part of the agreement. The load consisted of two bedrolls, cooking utensils, a flat copper skillet, and food, prunes, nuts, a sack of meal, tea, and a small skin of sweet wine. Azarias walked away into the dust of the yard for a moment and returned again. Tobias noted that he discreetly slipped what appeared to be a sword into a sheath sewn into the donkey's saddlebags. He did this as he checked to make sure the load was secured on the seasoned old donkey. The crowd vociferously, and loudly, offered advice even on these simple tasks. With everything now secure, they were ready to leave.

The sun was past the peak of noon as they made their way out of the great yard of the Caravansary to begin their journey. Every one, and it was now a sizable crowd, wished them God's speed, good fortune, a happy and safe journey, and timely return. The two men, one donkey, and a dog, headed out the city gate on the Assur Road, and were on their way.

* * *

Tobias and the Angel

By mid afternoon the little party was well past the environs and activity of Nineveh, past the military staging areas, past imperial cotton fields, past the corn and barley fields and heading on down the main highway. Tobias was beside himself; the trip itself, the pleasure of Azarias' company, and the hope of helping to end the long ordeal of his poor father, filled him with excitement, joy and a strong sense of purpose. That and he was released, at least for the time being, from the boring scribe school, the daily duties at the stand, and the sad tension in his home. Now he could forget the pinch of poverty, and be a man among men, on the road. He walked briskly on ahead, followed by the dog, then realized he had gotten far ahead of Azarias. He could have stopped and waited for Azarias and the donkey, but such was his enthusiasm and energy that he went back to them.

"You'll end up making two trips if you don't pace yourself," the wise guide suggested. Slowing down to keep pace with Azarias he twice stumbled. Azarias moved along at a more comfortable pace, tapping the rhythm of his walk with his "Moses staff", as he called it, a rattan rod a forearm taller than he. He nodded his head to Tobias indicating the rhythm, and to help him keep his pace. As the afternoon wore on Tobias caught on, and they walked along together.

Azarias called the donkey Saul -- "He is such an ass, after all." And Saul moved along slightly behind the two men, keeping up, reluctantly it seemed. He did seem to have been this way a time or two.

Nimrod, the dog, after having received a good kick from the donkey, for nipping at his hooves, gave Saul plenty of room and trotted along ahead of the pack, checking out trees and bushes, chasing an occasional ground squirrel, and stopping to scratch an occasional flea. Before they had been on the road many more hours, the four gave the impression of having been together a long time, and were a foursome set on a definite purpose.

Robert Wanless

The traffic on the road was mostly northbound, to Nineveh. Southbound traffic was more usual in the morning, and the bulk of it was on the Tigris, the flat *kelecs*, barges made of cedar logs, drifted easily on the river's southerly current, and while more expensive, and slower, it was preferable to the hotter, dustier, travel by road. And the road was well traveled and the traffic was such that one never felt lonely traveling on it. There were military convoys, caravans coming out of the Zagros Mountains, couriers, shepherds with flocks of sheep, swine, and cattle, going to market. There was camaraderie among the travelers. Other travelers looked at the foursome with looks bordering on admiration, recognizing them as people on a set and probably important purpose. Passing troupes of soldiers, caravans, and occasional groups of travelers, would nod greetings to them. Tobias soon felt he was a regular on this way, part of the traffic, an experienced traveler.

Azarias explained several times the route they would take over the next few days, finally drawing a rudimentary map. They would go on south down the Tigris River Road, for the next few days, going past the former capital of Nimrud, then past the ancient and titular capital of Assur, which stood across the river down where the Tigris widened. Past Assur, they would continue on south to the junction of the narrower river, the Little, or lower, Zab, a distance of about seventy miles from Nineveh. At the Little Zab they would head east up the Kirkuk Road, into the foothills, to the town of Arzuhina, then at Kirkuk, southeast on the older, but more direct, and dangerous, Robber's, or Smuggler's, Road -- it had both names. It was the mention of that road at the caravansary which got at least two of the kibitzers going, one advising against it, the other in favor, and he calling the other a coward, and they were soon nearly at blows. While it wasn't used as much as the main road, it was still used, by smaller, inter-mountain caravans, or ore packs, and mounted couriers looking to save a day or two.

But that was still ahead. In the meantime they would travel the main road, the River Highway. It was a good, wide smooth road, at least a tall man's height above the river bank. Dusty, of course, but one could always stop along the banks of the Tigris, and find ample resting areas by the lush reeds, rushes, and willows, and often grassy areas, shaded by willows and palms all of which drew their sustenance from the ancient river. At these places, like parks, one could rest and bath at the end of a day of travel, and pull one's dinner fresh and flipping from the river.

As they moved along in the afternoon sun, they passed a caravan heading north toward Nineveh and a troop of soldiers on patrol from Nineveh passed them. Then came a disreputable looking trio of men, a dirty, foreign-looking group, Scythians or Armenians. The fiercest of the three, a heavy set man, with thick arms covered with tattoos, and with bronze studded leather bracelets on each wrist, was riding a camel. This camel itself was decked out with black leather streamers, and shiny tin stars and crests. The two others with him rode tandem on a mule, a good-sized one, but poorly groomed. They were all dressed in leather and fur, and had pointed leather caps, with flaps down over their ears, even though it was a warm summer's day. Tobias noticed that all the men had Tattoos, and the fierce-looking one had a running footed cross on his forehead. He believed he had seen that fellow at the canteen in the caravansary. The three stared at our foursome, appraising them ominously, as they rode by at a fairly fast pace. They also elicited a growl from Nimrod, and a weary side-glance from Azarias. The second man on the mule turned to stare at them as they rode by. He had an evil kind of flat, open smile -- open because at least two of his front teeth were missing. Tobias said, after they were safely down the road: "They sure seem like a rough bunch."

"They try," said Azarias.

Tobias began thinking, as he walked along, that Azarias' opinion on the time the trip would take was beginning to seem optimistic in the extreme. But he did have that remarkable assurance about the way that he said things. If it would only take two days, maybe they ought to press on till dark, rest only briefly the first night and get on their way first thing the next morning.

It was late afternoon when they passed the Great Ziggurat at Nimrud, off to the east. It looked like an enormous brick oven, or forge, stained a bright golden yellow in the late afternoon sun. "The tower of Babel?" Tobias asked.

"One of them," Azarias answered.

By evening Tobias realized that pressing on till dark might be a lot harder than it sounded. In spite of his youthful vigor, he realized he was not going to be able to go on much longer this day. "Maybe we should stop and rest?"

"Not used to this much walking, huh? Yeah, well, you do look a bit tired. We're not going to find a place a lot nicer than this," indicating with his hand one of the many park-like rests along the riverbank. Here they stopped for the evening. Tobias removed the saddlebags from Saul, and tied him on a long rope to one of the Willows. With Azarias sitting next to him, Tobias, after a respectful time looking at the sun, a golden disk in a sky filled with scarlet clouds, lay back on the grassy bank, eating some dates and bread and took a swallow of sweet wine. He looked over and smiled at his friend and guide, then promptly fell asleep.

At the first sign of daylight, however, Tobias was wide awake, and showing the resiliency of youth. He jumped up, and greeted Azarias, who himself was already awake. A short snack, some grain to Saul, and a morning chase of a ground squirrel for Nimrod, and the foursome hit the road. The newness of the adventure had worn a bit when they stopped for the mid day meal, and by late afternoon when Tobias checked again on how far they had gone, it did seem they were making very good time. On they traveled enjoying the warm, dry, day and the breeze off the Tigris that was cooling and comfortable.

"Is this the way you normally go?" Tobias asked.

"I travel different ways."

"How many other ways are there to Rages. Surely you wouldn't want to take a longer way?"

"Toby, my boy, there is more than one way to make the trip."

Calling him by his nickname threw off his line of questioning. Also Azarias always spoke with such confidence that he was not inclined to argue or question him any further.

"You see how the river widens and deepens here? We are approaching Assur. If you look closely you can see it there, in the distance," and he pointed down the river to the southwest. "Assur was an unpleasant place, even at this distance, more fortress than city. As Assyria has grown in size and dominance of the rest of the world, the rulers no longer believed in the continued need for a fortress-capital. Assyria, they believed, was invulnerable," Azarias was explaining. Azarias was passing on this little Assyrian history lesson as they walked on. "Assur was hard to defend from the west. Not that they had much to fear from that direction. King Sargon just wanted something bigger and better. That and I think unjustly claiming his crown at Assur bothered what conscience he had. Much of the government had already moved on to Nimrud. Even Nimrud was better than Assur. Of course, Nimrud was only a stopping off place till Sargon could build his great fort. Well, in the end, Nineveh became the capital, and Assur remained as the first defensive point should the Babylonians cause trouble in the south -- which they probably will."

"How do you know all of this, Azarias?"

"I'm smart. And I have access to inside information."

Azarias was also smart enough to notice Tobias seemed to be tired again, and even though it was comparatively early, he said: "There are several comfortable looking spots to rest for the evening. I tell you what; we'll stop early. By tomorrow you should be able to keep up the pace."

Even though the boy was anxious to move on, he had to admit he was tired and his feet were burning. This was a good chance for him to rest his feet, and recover some strength. So, they halted at a grassy stretch about a hundred yards long, which sloped gently down to the river. There were clumps of willows as boundaries on both the north and south side of the spot. It was just above Assur, which they could see not far in the distance. The place, as Azarias indicated, would allow for a comfortable rest.

"This is the longest I have ever been on the road," said Tobias. "except when I was a babe and we came to Nineveh. I wish we could have afforded to rent a couple of camels."

"They're smelly, spit, and have lousy dispositions. Besides, walking is good for you. You'll feel better when you've washed the dust from your face, and soaked your feet in the water. Why don't you go down to the water there, soak your feet, and maybe even catch a nice Bass for your dinner."

"I've no seine with which to do so," Tobias said removing his sandals and sinking his feet into the cool water. He lay back on the bank and stretched out.

"I'll show you the way to catch the big ones," Azarias said and set about doing so.

Tobias sat up again and splashed water on his face liberally. Nimrod came up to him next and nuzzled him on the arm, then scampered over to a stick on the ground, picked it up in his teeth and dropped next to Tobias. Tobias took the hint and threw the stick out into the river, and Nimrod swiftly jumped in and swam after it, returning with it in his mouth.

Tobias and the Angel

Azarias, meanwhile, had walked over to the saddlebags lying under a willow tree, and took out a roll of twine. Then he found a length of stiff copper wire. He broke off a length about as long as his first finger. He bent one end of the wire around his thumb, and deftly bent the other end into a tiny circle. Through this little hole he pushed one end of the twine, tying it tightly. He walked back toward Tobias, and stopped for a moment. He looked down at the ground concentrating intently. Tobias watched all of this. 'What was Azarias doing,' he wondered. Azarias quickly bent down and plunged his right hand into the soft earth, reaching, as it were, under the grass, and pulled out a long, fat, squirming earthworm. He pushed the copper wire through one end of the worm, which arched and twisted, and then pushed the wire through the other end, then continued over to Tobias. He handed whole apparatus to him saying, "Here you are. Throw this end into the water as far as you can, and hold on to this end of the line. In no time you should have a nice dinner hooked on that end of the string. Then all you have to do is pull it in, and cook him."

Tobias took the fishing line and looked at it. He looked out into the water at Nimrod swimming back with the stick he had thrown again. Tobias thought he saw a light colored shadow following the dog in the water as the happy dog climbed back on the bank. Nimrod did a good nose-to-tail shake and produced a rainbow in the spray. Then he rolled on the grass and lay down, his head up and alert, to enjoy a rest.

Tobias threw the line out maybe twenty-five feet into the water. He watched it settle as he sat down on the bank to relax with his feet soaking in the water again. He inattentively held the line in his hand. It was only another moment before he suddenly jumped almost straight up pointing at the water aghast and yelling: "Merciful Heavens, Azarias! Did you see that? I think it was a fish!" He pulled in the line.

"They get pretty big in this section of the river," Azarias said calmly. "Well, don't just stand there. Why do you think I gave you that line with a fishhook on the end. Toss it out again, further."

Tobias pulled the line in. The worm was still on the hook, and he tossed it out farther into the water. This time he didn't sit down but stood concentrating on where it sank, wondering, half hoping, and in no time, or very little time anyway, something yanked on the line and almost pulled him into the river. Azarias watched as the boy suddenly cried out in fear: "Holy smokes, Azarias! If this is that fish I saw I'm in trouble!" He held onto the line that was cutting now into the skin of his hand. "I think I may have hooked a sea monster. He's as big as I am!"

Nimrod was up on his feet now. He scampered down to the riverbank in front of Tobias, darting back and forth at the water's edge, barking at the fish.

Tobias yelled over to Azarias, "He's enormous and I think he means mischief."

"Well, don't give him a lecture; pull him in! He's food for our journey -- and more! Don't let him get away!"

"I think he's planning on having me as food for his journey!" Nimrod, darting back and forth, continued barking fiercely. "Nimrod, get back! Azarias, I can't hold this line ... Line! It would take a rope to hold this beast!"

"Less talk, more effort!"

Nimrod stayed in front of Tobias running back and forth, his ears back, his tail twitching, barking.

"Shut up, dog! I've enough trouble listing to Azarias without having to listen to you too."

"Wait for him to surface again, and then loop the line around your wrist. Don't be afraid. Get on down into the water."

"Are you crazy, get into the water?"

Tobias and the Angel

"Yes, then, when he lunges for you, grab him by the gills and lift him up out of the water! Then you will have mastered him; break his neck, and pull him onto the land!"

"Azarias, will you come down ... shut up Nimrod! And get out of the way! Come down here and give me a hand with this thing!"

"Nimrod just wants to help!" Azarias offered, pleasantly.

"If the fish lunges at me he's likely to swallow me -- or the dumb dog. Wow, there he is again! LOOK AT HIM! I can't grab him. He's bigger than I am!"

"Of course you can grab him! Get back, Nimrod! You're the man; he's the fish. You're strong and you will master him!" Azarias, it should be pointed out, was standing this entire time leaning against the trunk of an enormous willow tree several yards up from the edge of the river, and calmly giving instructions. "Be bold now, and persevere. You'll have him ashore in no time."

Finally, the fish did go for him and with a loud grunt, Tobias had him. He worked first his one hand, then the other, into the opening of the gills, and with all his strength, lifted the fish up, out of the water. He found strength and twisted its head this way, then that, as he pulled it back up onto the bank. With another loud "ooff!" He pulled the fish up out of the water and onto the dry land. He stood for a moment, teetering off-balance, but proudly holding the fish up, but out away from him; then he suddenly fell down backwards onto the ground -- the fish on top of him. Nimrod rushed over to the fish, barking and hesitantly snapping at it.

"Nimrod, you numskull, cut it out. Help me Azarias. This fish is crushing me!"

"Nonsense. Just roll over, lad. Get out of the way, Nimrod."

Tobias did, and the fish flopped off him hitting the dog that yelped and darted out of the way. Tobias managed to get up onto his feet and quickly stood back away from the fish, as if it might have another go at him. He looked with amazement at the huge fish struggling on the ground. Nimrod too stood back a bit now, growling at the fish.

Azarias finally walked down toward Tobias: "Ha ha ho! What a good catch! A splendid fish, well worth the boweling! We'd better do this right away. I'll show you how to save the heart, gall and liver. They are what we call a sovereign remedy for numerous ailments. You can roast part of the meat which we will eat tonight, and salt the rest. Excellent provisions! This will serve us well when we reach the highlands in Media."

Azarias went to the willow and took a length of branch as long and as thick as his arm, handed it to Tobias and told him to hit the fish soundly on the head to end its suffering. Then he took his knife, handed it to Tobias, and talked him through the cleaning, scaling and filleting of the fish. Tobias took note that Azarias didn't actually do any of the work, only instructed him, but so well that he felt exactly as if he knew what he was doing. When he was done Azarias took salt from the bags, and showed how to salt the remaining fish. Then they started a fire and let it burn down to glowing coals. And when the color of the coals matched the setting sun, Tobias put a generous filet into the copper skillet, and cooked the fish in oil, and seasoned it with wild thyme and fresh dill. He served it with a garnish of watercress from a shallow stream that ran into the river.

As they ate Tobias began his questioning again. "Tell me, Azarias, what healing properties are in those parts of the fish you want me to save -- don't you think they may get a little smelly, by tomorrow?

"Maybe a little. But as the parts dry out it won't be too bad. It's heart has this characteristic: if it is laid on hot coals, like those that warm a bedroom, the smoke from it will rid man, or woman, of the harassment of a demon, or the effects of an evil spirit."

A demon or evil spirit, huh? Are there many demons and evil spirits in these parts?"

Some. It might even be a hot bed. Actually it's no worse than any other place. But up in the mountains, it's not good. Now, as for the liver, it makes a splendid salve for the healing of eyes especially those that have cataracts or a white film or patches binding them."

"You mean, like my father's?"

"Like your father's."

The sun was setting over the river beyond Assur as they ate their dinner, with Azarias only seeming to pick at his serving.

"Is the fish not to your liking?" Tobias asked looking at Azarias

"It is good, and there is a lot of it. I'm not a heavy eater." He changed the subject deftly, as he was inclined to do: "Tomorrow, or so, we'll be in Ecbatana. There we'll stay the night with a tribesman and fellow kinsman of yours, a not-too-distant cousin on your father's side. His name is Raguel."

"Tomorrow, or so?"

"Maybe the day after... it depends upon how well you do, and what we run into along the way."

"You have the most peculiar notions of time, Azarias. And what are we likely to run into?"

"Well, you get into the mountains you never can tell. There are wild animals, of course, and men who act like them."

They sat quietly while Tobias ate the rest of his dinner. Then as he became more and more drowsy, Azarias arose, bid the young man to say his prayers while he went to a place to say his own. Tobias quietly thanked God for the adventure, the good counsel of his friend Azarias, even for the dog, and old Saul, who certainly carried his share of the load. He asked God's blessing on his poor father and mother, but before he could say 'Amen' he was fast asleep.

Robert Wanless

Chapter 8
In the Zagros Mountains

"Wake up, Toby, my boy, time to rise, praise the Lord, and start the day. We've new adventures ahead of us. Nimrod, give Toby a good morning kiss." And the happy, frisky, obedient dog trotted over and licked the sleeping Tobias' face, which did the trick.

"Hey dog! Cut that out!" Tobias tried to turn away from the dog.

"Good dog. Just man's best friend showing some affection, Toby."

The morning sun had not appeared above the distant snow-covered peaks of the Zagros, but had colored them a ripe peach. After a breakfast of the cooked fish, served with bread and cold tea, the foursome was once again moving along the highway. Tobias had trouble watching the road ahead, because he couldn't take his eyes off the ominous fortress that was Assur across the smooth waters of the Tigris.

The river was nearly a mile across here and blue as it reflected the morning sky. Traffic was already plentiful, and playful shouts and greetings from kelec to kelec drifted across the water. Tobias began calculating that they did, in fact, seem to be making much better time than he had thought possible. Yet, strangely enough, they didn't seem to be moving all that fast. It would obviously take longer than the "couple of days" Azarias had first said it would take, but at the rate they were going it sure wouldn't be the ten or more days Tobias had expected.

By late morning they arrived at the junction of the Little Zab River and the Tigris. The Little or, best said, Lower Zab, was a couple of hundred yards across, deep and with swirling currents at the juncture. Here they could either turn left and head up to highlands on the north side of the river or pay to cross on a narrow pontoon like bridge. The bridge was a floater, built upon taradas, those handsome narrow boats of the marsh area to the south, old now with their long bows and sterns blunted. They were lashed together and thick boards laid across their beams. Not bad crossing, nor expensive for a man or two. But Azarias took them instead to one of several log barges used as ferries. There were several different sizes of these kelecs, smaller and flatter than the ones that traveled the Tigris. The skippers charged different rates for the crossing and these rates varied according to the number crossing and the tenacity of the bargainers.

The kelec Azarias chose was a smaller one that could hold a donkey and up to four men. It was poled across the river by its master, and his son, and steadied on its course by a thick guide rope stretching across the Zab and anchored on either side to thick posts planted deeply in the banks of the river. As Azarias began bargaining with the master, Tobias noticed his son had a lame leg, and stood by on the barge supported by his crutch.

"How much for the crossing, my good man?" Azarias asked, in a gentle playful voice.

"One silver shekel, sir, for the three of you. The dog rides for free."

Azarias looked at him a moment and said, "You don't understand, we only want to go to the other side of the Zab here, not all the way to Babylon."

"That's why I reduced the price to a mere shekel, sir -- even though I've a wife and a lame lad to feed with my earnings."

"A whole shekel does seem a lot, Azarias," Tobias whispered to his guide.

"This is just the opening game. Relax."

"How much if I heal the lad for you -- of course, I wouldn't want to cost you the sympathy business."

Tobias and the Angel

"I get little of that -- it offends my son. And how would you propose to heal my boy? While you look the part of one who could do most anything, you have none of the appurtenances of a physician."

"A physician's best tools are his knowledge. That, sir, I have in abundance."

"Well we've seen many a funny clothed physician, Sir, heard their chants, felt their compresses, smelled their salves and spent most of our money. And the boy's no better. If it's all the same, we'd just as soon eat from the toil of our labors, let the boy continue with the crutch, and watch you cross that wavy bridge yonder."

"You're a good and upright man," Azarias said to him, then turned and said: "Toby, go over to those sword plants on the riverbank. Break off a hand's length of a fat one and bring it to me." Then to the crippled lad Azarias said, "Sit you here upon this box, and extend your lame leg to me." And to the boy's father, "Sir, in the bag on this side of the donkey, you will find a roll of linen."

"Well, I'll probably regret it, but, heal away then and the passage will be my pay."

"Done. But, that includes passage back across when we pass this way from the other side in a fortnight?"

"If the leg is truly healed, agreed."

"Then bring me the linen."

To Tobias coming back with the cutting from the sword plant Azarias said, "Now, go to that palmetto bush there by the ramp; cut off a young pale green frond." Azarias then began to squeeze the spear from the sword plant and spread the juice from it on the boy's leg. Tobias handed him the Palmetto frond, and cutting the long hard stem part from the frond, he wrapped the leafy part around the leg. He then took the roll of narrow linen, stretched it out, and carefully, but not tightly, wound the linen strip over and around the frond, from the boy's ankle to midway up his thigh. Azarias admired his handiwork for a moment, stood, tussled the boy's hair, and said, "It will be a little uncomfortable for a couple of days. You'll have to keep your leg straight for that time." Then, turning to his father, "Remove the bandages on the Sabbath eve, and he'll be playing ball the next day."

"Sir, we're not Yisraelites. We don't keep the Sabbath."

"Doesn't matter. The Sabbath will keep you. Do as I say, and the boy will be healed."

"I've heard of your God, sir, and your rates are certainly less than the Assyrian physicians. We'll do as you say. If what you say comes true, you've free passage with me for as long as ever you come this way."

"Fair enough," said Azarias. With the boy staring at Azarias in admiration and trust, and the father smiling hopefully, Saul was led onto the raft, and with Nimrod standing at the bow, or the front anyway, barking a warning to fish and fowl, Tobias pushed off and they began crossing to the other side. The man still seemed a bit skeptical, but was smiling none the less, as he steadied the passage of the kelec by holding onto the thick rope, stretched across the river. The happy boy pushed on the long pole with what seemed renewed strength and vigor.

"Ferrymen usually quote you one price on one side of the river, then add a surcharge before you get to the other side," Azarias said to the man.

"Not this one," he returned. "And I've had men of the court, and military officers too, agree on one fare, then taxed me by half at the other side."

"Not this one. But, I'm from a higher court," said Azarias with a wink to the boy.

They reached the other side and the man thanked Azarias, profusely and sincerely. The foursome was sent on their way with thanks, and with faces beaming with trust.

Tobias and the Angel

On they headed, east along the much straighter road, up to the mountains. Tobias pondered all that had happened as they moved along; finally, a good distance from the crossing he asked, "Azarias, are you a physician?"

"Not in the normal sense of the word."

"How will what you did heal the boy?"

"What I did won't heal the boy. But, it won't hurt him either. God heals the boy. But the things we did help their minds and hearts adjust to the healing process. When next week he's as good as new, he'll scarcely remember how he had been, or how it all happened. But he'll be happy, and with a good father he'll be a good man."

The road began to climb. Tobias thought of many other questions he wanted to ask Azarias, but couldn't form them. How was it, for instance, they were making such good time? Where did he learn the healing arts? Why did the animals take to him so? Perhaps, he thought further, he didn't really want to know the answers.

As the day went on, the climb got steeper, and Tobias soon forgot the questions bothering him, in the interest of making their way and saving his breath. It was late afternoon when they had passed through the small mountain city of Arzuhima. They stayed the night on the outskirts of town, in the open area outside a small inn.

Arising the next morning, and getting on the road again, Azarias said, pointing to a road leading off to their right, "Here is where we take the short cut, to the old Smugglers' Road." The road, on which they departed from the broader, smoother road was a well-rutted mining road that lead off to the tin and copper mines deeper in the mountains. It appeared, at first, every bit as much used as the other road. But within a mile or so it was apparent that the road was used as much but differently.

"This road is no longer under Assyrian control?" Tobias asked.

"It is under the control of the Medes, as much as it is under the control of any government."

Tobias was quiet as they made their way along; finally he asked, "What if we run into bandits or ... well, we are not armed."

"We have the armor of God. His grace is a shield and a buckler!" Azarias answered.

The young man said nothing, but he cast a side-glance at his strange guide and friend. Was he teasing? "Well, be that as it may, Joshua and David too, armed themselves with swords. Even Samson used a weapon (in deference to Saul he didn't mention the infamous jawbone). If we are going to take a dangerous route don't you think a good sling, or broad sword, might be advisable."

"Don't you trust me, Toby? Anyway, from the way I remember this route, brigands were pretty far down the list of things to be afraid of. How do mountain lions and bears rank in your list of fearful things?"

"Azarias, I am only a young man. My parents depend on..."

"I know; I know. But, tell me, can you use a sling or a broad sword? You're a city boy, remember?"

"I've practiced with a sling some ... and I would like to learn to use the sword. That's why I want to go to officers' school. I don't want to have to be afraid all of the time."

"Toby, you're paying me good money to get you to Rages and back -- or at least your father promised to pay me good money. Do you think I would deliberately, or even irresponsibly wreck my chances of earning good, or even bad, money? Really!" And giving Saul's bridal a yank, and patting Nimrod on the haunches, the tall guide gave a "Tsk--Tsk!" and pressed on his way. Tobias followed shamefacedly.

The road soon showed lack of maintenance. And there was less traffic now, only an occasional farmer with a load of forage or manure; a shepherd with a flock walking along or crossing

Tobias and the Angel

the roadway; women, in pairs, often with a couple of children in tow, going to or coming back from errands. Grass and weeds were common now, even rather high, and there were holes, and gullies in the roadway and places where slides had either covered or washed away parts of the road surface.

As they continued the climb the air became dryer, if not appreciably cooler. By late afternoon a breeze had picked up, or rather started down, from the highlands. On their way they passed an occasional village or hamlet, a random collection of round mud huts with rounded roofs, some lean-tos of simple timber branches with qasab mats laid over them and coated with mud dried to hardened stucco. These were often in shallow valleys, or on plateaus, small villages that were only a gathering of a tribe, shepherds and their families, inhabited from early spring to mid fall. Arriving for the fresh mountain grass, then as the mountain weather degenerated with the coming of winter, these people migrated back to the agricultural villages in the more temperate foothills, or the lowlands nearer the Tigris.

Tobias didn't talk much now. He became mesmerized with all that was around him, drinking in the beauty of the mountains. The strange light in the mountains enchanted him, their limestone make-up played with the light, and at the different hours of the day it changed color, playing off the cliff faces, stones, and boulders. The morning grays and purples gave way at midday to a bright golden shimmering glow. Another light and color show awaited them in the evening. The mountains had their own peculiar sounds: the echoing calls of birds of song and prey, carried on the breezes and mixed with the rumble of waters rushing in the streams that fell along below them into the gorges. Sometimes too there were periods of what might be best described as majestic quiet. But it would be pierced with an equally majestic cut, as a bird of prey would drop with a scream, terrorizing its prey. As they got higher the vegetation changed from the ash, pine and pin oak forests below, to rich long-needled pine, then higher still to scrub pines. The grassy plateaus and valleys changed from the dense mountain pasture grass to a coarser grass.

The young man gazed about him at the magnificence of the valleys below, the steep rock faces dropping straight down from the road on which they walked. He felt his heart swelling within him as he savored the light, the sounds and the smells of the great mountains. He scarcely watched the roadway as he moved, his head looking to his left and down, around in a wide arc, lifting his eyes as he turned his head up, looking beside the road and continuing up to the sheer cliff face on his right. The road took a sudden fairly sharp turn to the right, hugging the sheer cliff, and affording a view of still another valley down and out before them. Tobit was entranced by the magnificent beauty all around him. But then he suddenly stopped and gasped. There, maybe three meters above the road, standing on a promontory of jagged rock jutting out of the sheer cliff face, and right in front of him, was a mountain lion. It took a second or two for Tobias to realize what it was. The big cat was staring right at him.

In reaction he stepped back, and to the side. But he was standing too close to the edge of the road, and stepped into a small washed out at the edge. He lost his footing and not so much fell but slid down the side landing on a narrow ledge, several feet below. This startled the big cat, as well as the young man's companions.

"Azarias! Help!" Tobias shouted from below.

Azarias had looked up and seen the lion the same instant as Tobias had. And the lion was as stunned as everyone else was by the noise, dust and confusion. He had positioned himself into a crouch and ready to pounce, but seemed confused now as to which would be the target.

Nimrod too, at the same instant, looked up and saw the lion, its back arched and poised. Nimrod didn't wait, but ran to the

Tobias and the Angel

base of the promontory and began barking fiercely up at the big cat. The cat answered with an even louder and fiercer hissing roar that for a moment, anyway, daunted the dog.

Azarias looked to where the boy had dropped and rushed forward with his Moses staff at the ready and carefully watched the big cat, which Nimrod continued, louder now, to give a piece of his mind.

"Hey, Azarias, I'm down here!" Tobias yelled from the narrow ledge below, parts of which began breaking away from the cliff face. Tobias sneaked a look over the side. It was long drop down to a rushing mountain stream below. "Oops!" he said, then: "Hey, Azarias, give me a hand!"

But Azarias was more intent on diverting the cat's attention from Tobias, who, from where he was lying, was unable to see the cat, but very able to see the drop off just a few inches from his left side.

"Nimrod," Azarias said to the dog, "that cat's not afraid of you." The dog shot him a quick look which seemed to say 'mind your own business'. He wasn't backing down from any cat, not even one with a couple of hundred pound advantage on him. "Okay," Azarias said, ready to turn his attention to the boy, "if you think you can keep him at bay, then I'll go fishing for Toby."

The dog continued barking loudly, constantly feinting side to side, to divert the cat from calculating accurately its trajectory. He seemed, at the same time, to be trying to teach the cat an object lesson: 'it's not size, but will, that wins the day.' The cat shifted its attention briefly to the donkey. Over the years pack mules and donkeys had served as many a tasty meal; then to Azarias, who caused him some pause; but it was the dog to which it returned its attention.

Now Saul, the donkey, got into the act with his own commentary. Saul had lived long enough, and had been around enough, to know what one of these big lions of the mountains could do to a creature such as him. He knew that to stand docilely by was to become a meal. He began braying loudly, offering his evaluation of the situation. Soon he was not only braying, but even began bucking, and kicking his hind legs out. Azarias was briefly amazed at the energy the old boy was showing.

Meanwhile, Azarias called down, stealing a quick look over the edge to the boy lying rigid, "You okay down there?".

"I think so. But I'd rather be up there."

"You might want to think twice about that. Nothing broken?"

"I can't tell, and I'm afraid to stand up to check."

Keeping one eye on the cat, Azarias got down on his knees by the side of the road and extended his Moses staff down for Tobias to grab. And it was at that moment that the cat, with all its legendary quickness, lunged from its perch. And it was at that moment that Nimrod jumped to the side and up onto a bolder on the side of the cliff, clearing the cat's projected landing spot. The cat hit the target in a cloud of dust and a spray of gravel, exactly where the dog had been, and without the customary grace we're inclined to expect from a cat. It lost its footing on the loose stones of the road surface and ended up spread-eagled on the ground.

What happened next was something that amazed the dog and Azarias, to say nothing of the mountain lion: Saul, while braying with near ear-splitting shrillness, and in a tonal range particularly offensive to cats, had also been bucking and kicking with his hind legs. He had managed to get turned around also just as the cat landed. The cat, opting on settling the ancient rivalry with the dog, and trying to right itself from its embarrassing landing, got its splayed legs more or less under him and was just getting up. In that brief moment, when the cat used all its instinct and its intelligence, which on a good day wasn't considerable, to change course and target, Saul struck out with his hind most artillery and the hapless mountain cat felt the power of the humble donkey--and his accuracy. Saul landed a good kick broadside on the cat. There was the muffled *whock!* of two well placed hooves hitting in unison, and the *crack!* of several of the cat's ribs, and the *Meeeooooowh!* of a hurt mountain lion--followed by a brief moment of silence.

Then the cat looked first at the donkey, then at the dog, then over at Azarias, then back up at the promontory. Azarias was up now on his knees, his staff raised. Without an instant of further hesitation, its legs grabbing for traction, slipping and digging at loose stones, the cat began running as fast as its painful side would allow, down the road a short distance, away from the fearsome foursome, then down an embankment and out of sight.

Nimrod, never one to let well enough alone, took off after the cat, at least as far as the place where it had disappeared down the embankment. He continued barking as loudly as before, but with a change of tone that clearly seemed a warning to the cat to stay away in the future.

"Help?" Tobias called from the ledge below to remind Azarias.

"Of course," said Azarias, once again extending his Moses staff, Tobias grabbed the end of it and was pulled up to safety. Shaken and nervous, Tobias began dusting himself off.

"That's the wild animal; would you like to try some bandits?"

Both Azarias and Tobias rewarded Saul and Nimrod with extra rations, warm pats and hugs, and many kind words as the foursome continued on their way to Rages. Tobias felt now a warm and common bond not only with his guide, but also with the animals.

Robert Wanless

Chapter 9
Through the needle's eye

It was later, that same afternoon, that the four passed through a small village situated at a crossroad. When this had been one of the main trade routes out of Ecbatana, the village had a popular rest stop for caravans. The new route to the north and the reduced Assyrian control of the area had its influence.

The road that crossed the road they were on was a secondary route, a narrow inter-mountain road used by farmers, miners, and other people of the area in their daily tasks, well used none-the-less. But, with most traffic now using the main route and even local suppliers and miners directing their activities to the new route further north, the village had become run down. It was a collection of stone and adobe huts, many of which seemed abandoned. There were only two large buildings, one a more or less vacant government post, which had housed maybe a company of soldiers and other officials. Further along the road they came within a dozen yards of the other building. It was the old caravansary. It seemed rather large and out of place for the area especially now. The building was comprised of an enclosed section of more or less two stories and a large open garage or stable. This opened to the left side where there was a staging or dismounting area with the remains of racks and tables used for removing cargo and spelling the animals. All this stretched around to the rear of the building proper. By the looks of things it had been a few years since any of this had been used. Tobias could see around to the right of the building, a corral with several animals, a camel, two mules, and a horse. Standing in the grassy area around the corral was a goat quietly munching on some grass. The front, they could see, was the inn and tavern, and though still in use, it was not in good condition.

The front wall was cracked and damaged which could be seen through the arches of the front porch or loggia. In front of the tavern were two rough looking men. One was leaning against the entranceway, the other squatting beside him. They mumbled something to each other as our foursome walked slowly by them. One of the men laughed out loud with a malicious and raucous laugh.

Nimrod didn't think much of the pair, and maintained a snarling, grumbling sound, eying them suspiciously and even showing his teeth, as they continued on their way. One of the men--the one with a long, wide strip of leather draped over his head, down onto his shoulders, and with armholes from which his tattooed arms protruded-- seemed familiar to Tobias. Where would he have seen such a person, he wondered as they continued on their way. Tobias turned to look back at him and remembered seeing the one man first at the caravansary in Nineveh, then later, with two different men, one the big fellow, with even more tattoos including one on his forehead, riding on a camel. They had passed them the first day along the River Road. One of the fellows was returning Tobias' stare, adding a sly, snide smile, and looking directly into Tobias' eyes. Tobias turned away quickly.

Azarias, without looking at Tobias, said, "don't turn your eyes away when you're in a stare down with someone; especially someone like that. If you once start, stay with it. But remember to smile."

"Well, I have to look where I'm going. Suppose I stumble over something? Anyway, I was as much looking at that tavern. I thought that maybe we could have stopped in the tavern for refreshment."

"You've no need of what they sell."

Tobias looked back again. A momentary flash of light came from the doorway and caught his attention. There was a figure standing in the doorway -- a bit of sunlight reflected off a knife

Tobias and the Angel

the man was using to pick his teeth. The other two men, who had been outside, weren't there now and had probably, he thought, gone into the tavern. So the foursome continued on past the little town, southeast on the old main road, now called the Robbers' Road.

Once outside the town the road began to narrow somewhat and grow steeper still. It was late afternoon now and the sun was warm on their backs, the road hard on their feet, the air thin in their lungs. The road hugged the edge of a long narrow ridge, dropping off and down to a dry riverbed a hundred feet or so below. Nimrod stayed close to the wall of the ridge rising sharply to their right, as did Saul, the donkey. Tobias, however, stayed to the middle of the road, occasionally testing himself by moving closer to the edge and looking down. Azarias kept an eye on him and watched the others, staying alert for danger.

Another hour or so and coming around a bend in the road, they saw, a hundred yards ahead, a needle's eye. These geological nuisances are the bane of caravan masters and a pain in the neck (and back) to caravans. These "eyes" are actually narrow openings in steep cliffs or promontories blocking the roadway. And some actually look almost like the "eye" in a needle. But most often they are cuts made through the blockage. Sometimes they are caused by rock slides, earthquakes, or weather. Sometimes, though, the granite is so dense road builders can't cut through to eliminate them, at least totally, so they are cut out the best the road builders can.

When a caravan comes upon a needle's eye, depending on the size of the opening, loads or parts of the load have to be removed from the beasts and passed through the opening by hand. The animals are then led through the 'eye,' and reloaded again on the other side. Depending on the length of the caravan, and the nature of the load, this operation can take up to a whole day.

From where he was walking Tobias, could see not only the needle's eye but also up ahead, as the road went round a protrusion just beyond the needle, he could see movement. He called it to the attention of Azarias, "Azarias, there appears to be others coming toward us on the other side of the eye."

"Yes. We'll let them have the right of way -- descenders over ascenders is the rule of the road. But, be alert."

The others waited quietly on the other side of the eye. Azarias and Tobias waited on their side. Nimrod began growling again.

"Quiet boy," Azarias said to the dog. Addressing the other travelers, he said louder: "You've the right away," he said first in Akkadian, then again in Mede, and was about to repeat it again in Hebrew, when an answer, in heavily accented Median, came: "It will be to our honor to let you have the right away."

"That's trouble," said Azarias. "The old robbers trick;" he spoke softly, "we unload and pass the goods through, then they grab it and hit the road. Robbers often kill one or two to strike fear in the caravan master."

He spoke again to those on the other side of the eye. "Please, permit us the honor of granting you the right of way, as it is yours by common right."

"No, your most Excellency, the honor is to be ours ..."

So they stood, either party, on either side of the needle's eye, for what was beginning to seem a long time. And all the time nobody said anything. Tobias was beginning to feel apprehensive and began to wish he knew how to fight with a sword. Azarias, on the other hand, stood with that curious, ironic smile which often accompanied one of his little comments, spread across his handsome face.

"What are we going to do?" Tobias whispered.

"Watch." Azarias answered. Then to the others: "Good sirs, we've all the time in the world."

Tobias and the Angel

Tobias was shocked at this, turned and whispered to Azarias, "What are you talking about, Azarias. We don't have …"

"Shusssh." Finally, Azarias walked brazenly through the eye and stood face to face with the leader. He spoke: "Ah! Well, it seems you've not as much to pass through, good sirs. And that you are probably in need of rest. This mountain air can sap your strength when you're not used to it."

There were three men. The leader was the big man with the tattoos, whom Tobias had seen in Nineveh, on the road and at the tavern. He just stood facing Azarias. Azarias smiled at them in a way that seemed almost kindly, but implied a serious threat. "I think you'll let us pass safely."

"And why would we not?" Asked the leader. The other men chuckled among themselves.

Azarias turned and looked through the eye at Tobias. "Come along now, Tobias, we've a way to go before we rest." Tobias handed Azarias the donkey's saddle bags, the bedrolls, and then he stepped through. Then he held the donkey's lead rope in his hand and began pulling the donkey. As Saul's head passed through the eye, Nimrod, who was standing behind the donkey, suddenly began barking at the men. This startled the donkey, which lunged through the eye and bumped into Tobias, knocking him down.

The men watching this began laughing. An embarrassed Tobias picked himself up and dusted himself off. "Stupid dog!" Tobias said. Azarias helped Tobias load everything back on the donkey and they were on their way again.

Tobias looked at the fellow he had been in the stare down with back at the inn, and said, "It was very kind of you to be so thoughtful."

"I would be careful if I was you," said the leader. "You might be wise getting some protection along this route. There are some dangerous characters, to say nothing of wild beasts."

"We'll certainly give it some thought ... it might be hard to find someone along the way here who could be trusted," Azarias said, again with his sly smile.

They had only gone a few yards when Nimrod turned around and started barking threateningly at the men. One of the men picked up a rock and threw it at the dog. Nimrod deftly sidestepped the missile and continued barking at them as they went on their way.

"That was scary. I thought we were going to have a fight on our hands," Tobias said when they were safely out of hearing. "I think I would like that." And he took a swing with an imaginary sword at the idea of someone in front of him.

"You may yet get your chance. They were just sizing us up," Azarias answered.

Tobias looked at his guide out of the corner of his eye. "You think so?"

"We'll see."

They continued on along the narrow mountain road. As the afternoon wore on the sun got lower, the colors changed to a bright orange, the air got cooler, and there seemed an inexplicable tension or suspense. Neither Tobias nor Azarias spoke, even Nimrod trotted along quietly. Finally Tobias broke the silence, "Where will we spend the night, Azarias?"

"The road widens along the way before we reach The Old Man."

"The old man?"

"That's the name of the largest peak on this ridge. Before the road starts up to it, there is a good rest area there. It has been popular in the past. Caravans would often stop and spend the night. It was cheaper than staying at a caravansary, or one of those commercial inns." And Azarias went on about traveling the trade routes. "At these stops," he went on "people would exchange gossip, sell each other food and treats. Sometimes in the summer, there would be music and dancing in the evening;

all in all there were some rather pleasant evenings in the late spring through early fall."

"Now?"

"On the main routes still. Here? We'll see. There could always be a lot more activity now."

The golden light of the day turned first to brilliant orange then to a burnt umber. The sometimes gusty breezes of the day became pleasant zephyrs, and as the birds began their evensong, the foursome came to the resting-place Azarias had mentioned. The road gradually widened into a large, flat, open area. To the right, as they entered upon this space, a steep cliff rose to nearly seventy feet above. To the left of the area, there was a drop an even greater distance to a gourge below. Water was available from a mountain spring which dropped carelessly down several levels over large limestone boulders to form a small pool at the base of the cliff, thence a stream which disappeared down the back of the clearing. The spring bubbled fresh water for people and the pool for watering the animals.

A small caravan, one of the innumerable inter mountain caravans, had already pulled into the clearing for the evening. It seemed to have been there a while. There were several dozen donkeys and mules, a dozen adults and four or five children -- it was hard to count them since they were running around between the donkeys chasing each other. Several men looked like caravaners, the others looked like mountain people, merchants probably, and tradesmen, their women traveling along with them and their children too.

Azarias waved at the caravan master with a friendly wave of the hand. The man waved back cautiously.

"Are you always this friendly with other travelers?" Azarias asked.

"It's wise and prudent to be so when traveling on this road," the man replied.

Along the base of the ridge, which rose above the clearing, were comparatively large scrub pines. Two grew near the spring that bubbled out the cold, but tasty, mountain water into the small pool. Azarias signaled Tobias to lead Saul over to the pine farthest from the caravan, but still close to the spring.

"We should have everything we need here. We're protected from wind; there's company if we want it and a good clear area to see what is about. Remove Saul's bags and you can begin preparing your dinner," he said to Tobias.

They unloaded the donkey and let him amble over to munch on the grass at the edge of the clearing. Nimrod checked out, then marked each of the pines in order; he played some tag with two of the older children in the caravan, then trotted back.

Azarias showed Tobias how to soak the salted fish in a pan of fresh water, prior to cooking it. They walked over to borrow some glowing coals from the caravan. In a short time they had a bright smoky fire going. Tobias watched as the fish cooked on the little fire. Smelling the cooking fish he thought first of his mother -- he really missed her; then thought of the drying fish gall for his father. He felt at peace, but still looked forward to getting the money and returning home to them. He would do all that he could to help his father, and maybe even see him healed of his affliction.

Azarias sat quietly on a rock a short way from Tobias and the animals, staring off into space. There was a little breeze and the sound of water, a chorus of birds completed their evensong, and from the caravan came the pleasant chatter of the other people. It was still light and quiet.

Nimrod growling at another party coming toward the clearing disturbed the stillness. A party of five came noisily into the clearing, one on a camel and two each on two mules. Tobias immediately recognized three of the men from the afternoon encounter at the needle's eye, the other two from the river road a few days back. As they got closer Tobias could see they seemed

Tobias and the Angel

even tougher looking than before. They had the eyes of men from the distant eastern mountains, and men who had been drinking-- Scythians, probably. They came to a halt and dismounted in the center of the clearing. They stood together talking, the biggest of the men giving instructions, gesticulating in various directions, the others glancing first at the foursome, then over to the caravan.

Azarias stood up, but made no other move. The men looked like they would come first over to Tobias, then looking at Azarias, staring at them, they went instead, over to the caravan. Azarias walked over to Tobias and said, "The Zagros Protection Company." He watched the men talk among themselves as they walked, slowly and threateningly, to the caravan. Two of them were laughing and making comments in the patois of the mountain people in this area. They were swaggering in feigned nonchalance, stopping again and talking together in a group.

Azarias said: "Toby, go to the saddlebags and fetch my sword."

"Yes sir," Tobias heard himself reply. It was the first time he had addressed Azarias that formally, but it was the first time he remembered Azarias giving an order. Azarias had the authority of a military officer. Tobias hurried over to the bags. Tobias remembered when loading Saul for the journey seeing what he thought was a sword, and sure enough, sewn into the top part of the saddlebags where they joined the part that rested on the donkey's back, was a scabbard. A flap covered the handle of the sword. He grabbed the handle and extracted the sword. It was beautiful. The handle was gold, inlaid with silver, beautifully crafted. He was surprised at how light it was. He had expected swords, especially ones of such size, to be almost too heavy for him to pick up. He admired the gleam of the blade and felt his heart quicken as he took a couple of quick sweeps with it. "If only I could learn to use a weapon like this," he thought as he walked back over to Azarias and handed the sword to him --

blade first. Azarias indicated with his head to turn the sword around and said, "Handle first. Always hand a sword or knife handle first."

Tobias did. Azarias took the sword by its handle and let the blade drop to his side.

Nimrod had moved over to Azarias now. He wasn't barking or growling. He just stood there with his tail twitching left then right.

The leader of the Zagros Protection Company, as Azarias had called the group, looked over at Azarias and said something to the other men. They all laughed. Then the man contemptuously turned his head away, and the group spread out and with the leader in front, they continued and reached the caravan.

"Come along, Toby, we may have to offer some assistance."

Tobias felt his chest swell. He wasn't sure what he could do, but felt that with Azarias, he would try anything. Just to be thought worthy to assist in something like this was the stuff of his dreams. He and Azarias walked slowly, and carefully, over to where the group of five was standing talking to the caravan master. The master at first seemed a little defiant, but his confidence waned and he began to seem frightened.

"They're offering protection to the caravan," Azarias said to Tobias. When they were only a few yards away, he spoke out aloud: "Now I see what you're about, my esteemed friends from the needle's eye: you're offering these good people protection. From what would you be offering protection? Perhaps you know of some disreputable, cowardly, slimy bandits that are known to infest these roads?"

The heavyset man, the one with the running cross on his forehead, turned to Azarias, "What's that you're saying, pretty one?"

Tobias and the Angel

"That's funny, I was sure that I had your patois down pat-- pardon that one. I was questioning the wisdom of your selling these people something of which they have no need."

"What the hell do you know about these people's needs? It looks to me like you need some protection from your hairdresser!" And the five burst out laughing. "You better get back out of the way. You're disturbing us. We'll take care of you in a few minutes."

Azarias without saying another word quietly raised his sword, pointing it at the leader. One of the men, a particularly foul-looking man, with only three teeth in the front of his mouth, and long mustaches snaking down either side of his mouth, pulled a long and particularly dangerous looking knife from out of his robe.

Tobias realized at that point he was totally unarmed -- and on quick reflection it was just as well, since he hadn't the foggiest notion about what he would do if he had been armed. But the foul looking man was approaching him. Azarias took a quick, very long step over to intercept the man, and with a dazzlingly quick move of his blade, caught the man's long knife blade, turned it and his hand around until he dropped it. Azarias then with another quick action, made a slice on the back of the man's hand. It was only a slight, but a very painful, 'paper cut' on the back of his hand, but it did hit one of the main blood vessels and began bleeding profusely. "Ow!" Said the man. "Look what you've done to me. And I'm unarmed!"

Which, of course he was, having dropped his weapon. The man stopped, and looked in amazement at Azarias. He started to stoop to retrieve the knife.

"Better leave it where it lays," Azarias said softly. The man pressed the injured hand against his long and dirty robe, while staring at Azarias with a mixture of hurt and awe. Tobias looked over at another man, the one with whom he had lost the staring contest earlier in the day. He began moving toward

Tobias. Tobias could also see out of the corner of his eye that Nimrod was also moving toward the man. Meanwhile, the big man, the leader, began walking toward Azarias, and the one who seemed to be the leader's lieutenant, was drawing his sword. It was a tense moment, but one with a lot of movement.

Tobias seeing that he had to do something, lunged toward the long knife lying on the ground. As he grabbed it, Nimrod jumped at the throat of the man who had been moving toward Tobias. The man who had dropped the knife and whose hand was bleeding, tried to jump back, but tripped on his long robe and fell over backward onto the ground, putting his other hand back to catch or break his fall, landed on it, painfully twisting his wrist.

The lieutenant who had pulled his broad sword was speeding toward Azarias. Azarias quickly brought his sword up to deflect the oncoming broad sword blade and with one quick flip of his wrist, had the sword out of the man's hand and on the ground. The leader was also moving with an angry, fierce expression on his face, charging to drive his sword into Tobias' chest. But Tobias was so filled with adrenaline he felt like he could fly if he wanted to. He jumped aside quicker than he ever realized he could and the man charging him tripped over Nimrod, who was on his way over to take a bite out of the backside of the lieutenant stooping down to pick up his sword.

The whole crazy dance had taken maybe thirty seconds, but when it was over here's the way it looked: three men were laying on the ground, two with painful dog bites (one on his neck, the other on his backside) the third with a sprained wrist and a bleeding hand. The two remaining standing were unarmed, and not a little afraid. Tobias and Azarias were both standing holding swords, while Nimrod was staring and growling fiercely at the leader who was lying prone on the dusty, rocky ground.

Tobias and the Angel

Azarias was the first to speak: "I don't know; if you fellows had this much trouble with just the two of us, and a nice little doggie, aren't you glad we got to you before you tangled with those people in the caravan?"

None of the men said anything. The people from the caravan began inching toward the fight scene, now that the battle was apparently over. Azarias went on, "Oh I get it. You were going to them to get protection from us?" Turning to Tobias, he went on "That's what it was all about, Toby, my boy. You were right, and I was wrong." Turning now to the group leader, he said,"Now, let me tell you what I'm going to do for you. I'm going to count to ten ..." Azarias looked at the leader, then at the others, questioningly. "You think that might be too high? I don't suppose any of you get into higher mathematics. Okay, I'll count to five (he held up the fingers of his hand to illustrate the number to which he would count.) -- we'll make that your lucky number, and if you are on the road before I get to five, he wiggled his fingers at them, you should be able to get back home safely.

"One..." He held up his little finger, and the men jumped up the best they could and began scrambling for their animals. "Two..." another finger illustrated. The lieutenant, stopping after a few yards, turned to come back as if for his sword. Azarias said, indicating he knew what he wanted: "Three! My friend here will keep it for you. That way you're not as likely to hurt yourself. Four!" And The Zagros Protection Company mounted up, and as Azarias said "Five!". "Starting tomorrow, I think you fellows should start looking for another line of work." They galloped down the road and away. The people with the caravan began clapping their hands in appreciation. The master walked over and invited Azarias and Tobias to join them for dinner of some kind of roasted animal. Tobias looked at Azarias and he assured him it would be good for the young man to eat. They served also a kasha seasoned with hot spices, peppers, and mountain onions with truffles. While Tobias couldn't understand the people, he sat and ate with them, smiling, and nodding at the presumed kind things they were saying; several of the men, and the boys acted out the sword fight over and over. Tobias was happier than he could ever remember being. He imagined that it might be fun were the Zagros Protection Company to visit them again.

Later Tobias and Azarias returned to Saul, and the grassy area where the good, brave donkey rested. They lay back on their bedrolls. Nimrod lay down next to Tobias and put his head in his lap. And in the silence of the cool mountain air, Tobias too went to sleep, and slept well that night, better than he could remember ever having slept before.

.

Chapter 10
Ecbatana

Ecbatana is first and best seen when approaching it from the west and seen from high on the ridge that is the northwest boundary of the valley in which the ancient city is situated. This is a magnificent panorama and is seen all at once as you come round a bend on the old route, the Robbers' Road, on which the foursome traveled. The peak which the road circumvents is called, by travelers and residents alike, *The Falcon* and opinions are divided as to reason for this name. Viewed from a certain angle and in a certain light, the mountain could resemble a falcon in flight. Another story is that falcons had nested on the lower part of the ridge and fed off the abundant wildlife in the valley. Anyway, the road rounds the peak and spreads out, curving gently following the contours of the mountain, and forms a natural overlook, before beginning its descent to the city below. This lookout is called The Falcon Look.

Seen from this high point the city is unusual. It is circular, and cities are rarely that way. And it is in the middle of the high, beautiful valley surrounded by snow-covered peaks. The heady fragrance of the valley wafts up to the heights born on the ever-present breeze that blows from the southeast. Before the new main road opened, everyone stopped at the Falcon Look to catch his breath, and admire the magnificent view.

Arriving at this overlook late the next morning, Azarias stopped and spread his hand with a flourish out over the magnificent valley below and said, "There it is Toby, my boy, beautiful Ecbatana."

Beautiful Ecbatana, indeed. Young as cities in this area go, it is said to have been "discovered" by King Deioces, and it was given its name by his wife, who was said to have been a Hebrew woman. But, in truth, the city had been around a good many years before King Deioces "discovered" it. Like Nineveh it grew in the beginning from a sound agricultural base. Later, its geographic location, in the middle of several trade routes, contributed to greater growth from the need for a place to rest and refresh of the ever-increasing caravans' going through it.

The city grew also because of its proximity to the numerous copper mines in the southern Zagros mountains and the various smaller mines which were the source of jewels, Lapis Lazuli mines being the most proximate. Ecbatana just continued becoming richer while its comparative isolation allowed it to keep its identity. The comparative isolation of the city was the result of its being in a high, long and fertile valley. And while it was on trade routes, it was not on any routes to military advantage. It became the capital city of Media, and in later years the summer retreat of numerous other kingdoms to the south and west.

Agriculture provided virtually all the inhabitants rich and varied diets, the mountains provided the rest: water, protection from excessive summer heat, and winter's worst winds; jewels and ore for working or selling, ample stone for the high and wide city walls. What else was lacking was supplied by the numerous caravans.

From the "Falcon Look" Azarias and Tobias stood observing the magnificence below, the valley as a series of geometric patterns, resembling a clever quilt maker's use of textures and colors. At this time of year the primary colors are the greens of the fields, but there was a variety of beiges, golds, tans and browns, with highlights of red and yellow, all wonderful to see.

From the top, and working one's way down the mountain road, the descent begins with juniper bushes, larger than what you are used to. They are in abundance higher up the mountain road, helping to make the initial decent even more fragrant. The greens change further down the road passing through a plateau

Tobias and the Angel

of dark green Pin Oaks, which offer shaded rest stops and groves. Lower down still come the vineyards, planted by some of the earliest Hebrew merchants and artisans, who migrated here following the trade routes. They became enthralled with the beauty of the area, and stayed. These people came freely, not like the poor exiles or captives such as Tobit and his family. They brought vines from Lebanon and were already producing grapes for a rich, semi-sweet wine. Fields of cereal, wheat, barley, alfalfa and a small-eared corn, many well on their way now to the harvest ripeness, line the roads of the north and south approaches to the city.

There are only two gates in the city's wall, in spite of the large circumference of the wall; one opens at the south end of the city, for access to the Indus and south to Susa and Babylon, the other at the north, for access to Assyria and beyond.

Azarias said to Tobias, "I promise you'll find it well worth the traveling."

"But, we're heading to Rages, Azarias."

"There, too, but I think you'll find your heart's desire here."

Tobias wasn't sure exactly what the guide was talking about. He thought, reflecting on those words, that his "heart's desire", at least as far as he was aware, was the restoration of his father's fortunes, and especially his eyesight. But he didn't give it all much more thought, since Azarias, on reflection, often said things that didn't seem to make much sense. Azarias touched Tobias' shoulder and said, "Come let's sit for a few minutes while I tell you what awaits you."

Together they sat on a boulder on the edge of the road that dropped off sharply and overlooked the valley below. He went on, "Your father has a relative here in Ecbatana, and Raguel is his name.

"I've heard him mention this man."

"Good. Then you know he has a daughter, the only child of him and his wife, Edna?"

Tobias nodded vaguely, but said nothing. Azarias went on, "The girl's name is Sarah. She is sensible, brave, and very beautiful. Raguel, her father, is an honorable man and quite well off. Her mother, Edna, is the very picture of probity."

Tobias looked at Azarias who was staring out over the valley below, and said, "So far so good." Azarias paused in what he was saying, reflecting a moment. Then Tobias remembered something: "Wait a moment: Raguel has a daughter? Yes, of course, that Sarah! I've heard stories about this girl. As a matter of fact every Yisraeli family in and out of exile knows about her."

"Just gossip."

"Just gossip? Holy smokes, Azarias, isn't she the one who has been married four or five times…"

"Betrothed seven times."

"Alright, betrothed seven times! I have heard it said that every bridegroom that brought her to bed --(here he stopped and he ran his forefinger across his throat). But seven times! The gossip hasn't even kept up. Seven dead husbands! That does go a little beyond simple gossip. I mean, even allowing for the tendency to exaggerate reports -- reduce the incidents by half you still have more than three dead men -- and all after having gone to the bridal chamber with her. Why she's a regular praying mantis!"

"No. Actually, the mantis is impregnated before she devours her husband. This girl is still a virgin. So, relax. There's a lot more to the story. But let me tell you this, right at the start, if you'll listen to me…" Azarias waited for Tobias. With the young man's nod, he went on, "If you will claim this man's daughter's hand in marriage you can be heir to all that the man possesses -- not the least of which is his daughter. You have only to ask him, and by rights, under the law, the girl is yours. You are her last kinsman."

Tobias and the Angel

"Last kinsman. No wonder! And as a for the man's fortune: he has saved a fortune on dowries alone. Sure he'll give her to me. What's he got to lose? It's what I've got to lose that worries me. No thanks."

"Toby, my boy, I'm surprised at you. You had your first taste of adventure just yesterday and showed yourself to be a young man of courage, almost daring. Now, here you are quaking over the simple mating with a lovely maiden."

"A lovely maiden! -- And with such a reputation!"

The two remained quiet for a time. Azarias said nothing, only looking out into the distance with the faintest of smiles on his handsome face.

Tobias continued: "Well, to be fair, I have heard it said there was some kind of demon involved and that it was he who did in those poor fellows, if the tale be true. Of course, it does seem funny that this demon does her no harm -- I mean, it is kind of funny that he only kills any man who tries to come near her. Did I say 'funny?'"

"You said 'funny'," Azarias answered, then continued being quiet, almost pensive, again.

Tobias, calmer now, went on, "well, it isn't that I'm just afraid for myself. If the same thing were to happen to me -- well, it would go hard with those parents of mine. You know I am all the children they have, and they are old now. This could give them a cheerless passage to the grave. I mean, they are having trouble enough with my father's blindness. My mother having to work is as hard on him as his blindness. Then, he really caught my mother's wrath for sending me off with you."

"May I tell you the whole story then?" To Tobias' nod of assent, Azarias, went on, "That demon has power to hurt some others, but not you. This fiend feeds on lust, such as those who marry with no thought of God: the ones who are intent solely on bedding the girl as if they were horse or mule, brutes without reason. That can't be the way with you. If, or when, you have won the girl's heart, and she is truly thy bride, then, for three days, deny thyself her favors."

Tobias also looked off to the distant mountains, then as what Azarias said sank in, he said, "You mean put off the wedding night?"

"Not 'put off the wedding night', only the more common activities of the wedding night. And only for three nights. Let me explain the regimen: spend the first night with your bride but on that night you burn the heart of the fish which we have preserved and is in the saddle bag, on the warming coals. And the time you spend together that first night, you spend it all in prayer. That should drive the demon away."

Tobias considered this for a few moments. "Let me see if I have this right: Burn the heart of the fish on the warming coals -- in the bridal chamber -- on our wedding night? And spend the whole time together in prayer -- and that *should* drive the demon away?"

"Hu huh. Then, on the second night ..."

"Oh good, there's more ... Frankly, I would like it if you could use a more definitive term than *should*. What if burning fish-heart, and our prayers, of course, don't drive the demon away?"

"Then I will," Azarias added sharply. "I'll see to it. Now, on the second night, you shall enjoy unity with her, but with the company of the holy patriarchs."

Again Tobias considered what was said. "Let me see if I've got this right: the second night I spend with my new wife, and Abraham, Isaac, and Jacob."

"That's right. Then on the third night, you shall pray for the blessing of children."

"I thought there was a more effective method of begetting children..."

Azarias let that pass. "When the third night is past, then you take your bride to yourself, with the fear of the Lord upon thee,

Tobias and the Angel

moved rather by the hope of begetting children than by any lust; and, in the true line of Abraham, you shall have the joy of thy fatherhood."

Tobias was quiet for while, then: "The other," and here he paused for emphasis, "*seven* fellows, they didn't do this?"

"Not really. As a matter of fact, not at all. And a, well you see what happened? Now, I realize this isn't exactly what you probably had in mind for your wedding night."

"No, not exactly, not for my wedding night. But to tell you the truth, I guess I've scarcely thought of my wedding night at all. My father and mother married late, and I had rather thought to do the same after I had studied law, or if I could talk my father into it, officer's school."

"Toby, my lad, have no fear; Sarah was destined for you before the world was made. You it is who shall rescue her. You shall win her heart and she shall go with you. So, don't worry!" Azarias stood, clapped the young man on the shoulder in a comradely way, and said, "Well, then. We've more miles to travel. By mid day we shall be at Raguel's house. Tonight we will confirm everything. Tomorrow we will go on to Rages and get your father's money. Then, when we return to Ecbatana, you shall be wed, and then we shall all return to Nineveh, and to your parents, and, then I shall be paid, and be on my way."

"Azarias, I'm sorry if I don't seem to appreciate your matchmaking."

"That's all right right. You get used to it in my business."

"What exactly is your business, anyway?"

"You're seeing it. I'm a ... guide."

"But you seem to be able to do so much more, so many things. You speak all those languages, you fight like a warrior, it just ... It just makes me wonder."

"Life is full of wonders. Up now. Let's be on our way."

And pulling on Saul's reins, Tobias fell in behind Azarias, who was walking ahead behind Nimrod. As Tobias walked he began thinking of all that Azarias had said, and his mind, like all young men's minds; sampled in fantastical imaginings, beautiful maidens (What did Sarah look like? He tried to picture the most beautiful girl he had ever seen. Then he tried to picture someone more beautiful. He began to be filled with a desire to see this beautiful, but dangerous, woman). With his young man's heart filled with the dreams and hopes of life, inheriting riches, being an officer in the always successful Assyrian Army; all this was his -- all he had to do was to survive the wedding night. He would do it -- he hoped; no, not just 'hoped', he would! So he began whistling a merry song, from his heart, and in spite of the danger, his heart was set on seeing the beautiful Sarah, defeating the demon, and making her his own.

Chapter 11
Tobias meets the beautiful Sarah

Tobias soon passed Azarias and was walking along briskly, trying to act nonchalant, as he kept up with Nimrod. The foursome walked down the Great Ecbatana Highway past the oak woods, the vineyards, and the orchards, and finally the green and golden fields ripe with the summer's fruit, to the north city gate of Ecbatana. The young man's expectations were propelling him along almost at a run down the long descent. Such are the ways of the young in pursuit of dreams of love.

"Come on Azarias, you're slowing down."

"It's our friend, Saul, Toby, I'm afraid he doesn't share your enthusiasm for an express trip. Come on Saul, old fellow, not much farther and you can enjoy a good rest," Azarias said to the donkey. And the old beast seemed to take heart and actually moved along a bit faster.

Even considering that the girl, in all probability, might be worth the wait, Tobias couldn't. He was dying (then he quickly changed the adverb to "Anxious"), he had to admit, to see her. And though he was not without apprehension, of course, he took some comfort in that he knew he didn't have to commit himself. Further, even if Azarias thought she was so "beautiful", he was old (so reason those in their late teens or early twenties about those in their early thirties). What he may think of as "beautiful" is not necessarily what a young man would so think.

When, at last, they arrived at the city gates they stopped at the guards' station there. Azarias spoke with the Sergeant on duty, telling him where they were from, Nineveh, who they were, Israelites, and their destination and business, to visit a relative, Raguel, thence on to Rages. He summed up saying: "We're going straight to the house of Raguel to rest before going on."

The Sergeant heard him out, looked at Tobias, and said, "The old Hebrew, Raggy's house, huh?" He chuckled. "You bringing more bride fodder for the black widow, huh? Ha ha ha," then he and the two other enlisted men on duty with him all started laughing. "When will they ever learn?" He continued, and laughing he waved Tobias and Azarias on through, while the three enjoyed laughing and making risque remarks.

The men, dog and donkey, passed on through the city gate, trying to ignore the laughter behind them. Azarias continued talking to Tobias, loudly, as they walked along, to divert his attention from the laughter and comments at his expense. "We can rest at Raguel's, perhaps have dinner, maybe spend the night, and if you really want, we can be on the road first thing in the morning. Are you growing impatient?"

"I suppose I am a little anxious. The truth is I'm dying to (he paused again at that unfortunate metaphor adding:) I suppose that was a poor choice of words. Since you brought this whole thing up, I would like to satisfy my curiosity, is what I mean, just get this over with. I didn't mean that like it sounds."

They headed down the main boulevard toward the center of the city, where the king's palace, court buildings, the main market, and the caravansary were all located. After three blocks Azarias turned right onto a similarly wide road, which had large one and two story houses, some almost like palaces on either side. Raguel's house was at the end of the street, not far from the city walls, and certainly in one of the better sections of the city. The house was larger than Tobias had expected, rather like a small palace, in fact. Stopping in front of the house, and admiring the gleaming white stone front, trimmed with green stone around the front door, Tobias stopped and looked at amazement at the building. Azarias was about to say something about the house, but Tobias stopped him, and indicated in sign language to listen. There was the sound of music coming from a window on the second floor and around the side of the house. It

Tobias and the Angel

was a young woman singing; a beautiful voice accompanied by a harp. The song was sad, a ballad about lost love, probably -- he couldn't understand the words, which were sung in a language with which he was unfamiliar, but the melody, the sound of the voice, the beautiful harp, all left him dumbfounded.

"Listen to that singing, Azarias. It's as beautiful as an angel's."

"How do you know?" Azarias asked, grinning and pulling the bell cord on the door lintel, "She sings beautifully all right, but I don't think she is quite up to the angelic choirs."

The front door opened directly and an elderly servant greeted them. To the inquisitive raised eyebrows of the man Azarias said, brightly: "We greet you, sir, and seek our fellow kinsman, Raguel, in the name of the Most High!"

The old man, smiled and nodded his head, "He'll be out in the garden tending his roses. May I show you in, good sirs?"

The two followed the servant through the marble floored, white-walled foyer, which turned into the hallway running from the front door all the way through the large house to the back. Tobias looked into each of the large rooms as he passed them: the living room, a parlor, the dining room, and what appeared to be an office, with racks holding clay tablets, and bins with rolled papyrus. The hall in the front of the dining room widened, leading to other rooms, the stairs to the upper floor, and out to a courtyard. This large courtyard, or atrium, was bordered on three sides with columns, and the back opened out into a garden. The inner floor space was ringed with beautiful rose bushes. As they stepped out into the courtyard, Tobias noticed that the singing, coming from upstairs, had stopped. The servant, who led them into the courtyard, politely cleared his throat.

Kneeling on a cushion on the flat tile floor was a jolly looking fellow, a white-haired gentleman who appeared to be in his late fifties, gently turning the dirt around the roots of a particularly large bush. The bush was covered with roses; the famous *Black Rose of Babylon*-- not actually black but purple so deep in hue that at first glance it appeared black. The kneeling gentleman raised his head with a surprised look that quickly changed into a warm, bright, welcoming smile. Azarias went to his side directly, and aided the man to arise, saying: "We have come from Nineveh, my friend here and I, and are on our way to Rages. We are of the tribe of Naphtali, now living in captivity at Nineveh. We are fellow clansmen of thine."

"Well then, a hearty welcome to you both, friends. From Nineveh, are you? Yes. Yes, I have kinfolk there. I am glad to see you so well after so long a journey." The man called into the house: "Edna, my dear, come look! Come see if this young man here doesn't look like our kinsman Tobit?"

Edna, a stocky, robust, and smiling woman came out and joined the men with a smile as big as her husband's. She had a large curly crop of dark hair, with a curious and attractive band of silver gray growing in the front and combed back. Her blue veil framed her bright face. When she spoke she had one of those voices that seemed to begin almost as a bell and end with a soft twinkle. Looking at Tobias she said "He does just that. Where did you say they come from, my dear?"

"They are from Nineveh, my dear! Where good Tobit lives.

"Ooooooh! Then you must know our kinsman, Tobit?"

Tobias was having trouble containing his excitement and some of it burst out when he almost shouted: "Yes, we do!"

"Ahhhh! Is he well?"

"Shhhh! Mother, please," an embarrassed Raguel, cut in. "You know full well his troubles."

"Yes, good mother, he is alive and all considered, doing fairly well! He is my father."

Raguel clapped his hands together, and with tears, rushed over and hugged Tobias kissing him on both cheeks. "Your father! God bless you, my boy, son of a good and noble father.

Tobias and the Angel

Ah, what grievous news that so good and charitable a man has gone blind!"

At this both Raguel and his wife were overcome by the tragedy of the situation, and began to weep. The two comforted each other, then Tobias, with tender words of mercy.

Tobias whisper to Azarias out of the side of his mouth while the commiserating was going on, "Where's the girl?"

"Ah ha. Now you can't wait, can you?"

"Just curious."

Raguel suddenly collected himself and said to the old servant who had stood looking on with a gentle, benevolent smile: "Well, please pardon our manners. You've had a long trip. Jacob, old friend, go fetch the travelers a bowl of water to do their feet, and tell Rebeccah to bring some cooled and sweetened wine to quench their thirst. You have animals?"

"Yes, a donkey and our dog."

"Good, good, good. Then Jacob, some meal and water for their donkey -- and the dog, good sir -- he doesn't bite?"

"Only Tobias."

"Tobias bites?"

"Oh, no sir, the dog just bites Tobias. A little joke between us…"

"Then you may bring the dog in with you, Jacob." The old servant set about to do as he was bid.

While the conversation was taking place, Tobias kept sneaking looks around the courtyard, and through the opening in the back wall to the garden in back, into each of the doorways, trying to catch a glance, to see if the couple's daughter was around. From where he was standing he couldn't see the stairs, nor could he see if she was in any of the rooms. Azarias talked to Raguel in small talk about the beauty of Ecbatana and the surrounding mountains. Then Tobias heard music again, this time coming from downstairs, inside the house. She wasn't singing this time, that is, not a song, but it was music nonetheless, and from the same voice he had heard singing. It was the voice of a young woman, and talking now to -- Nimrod. Her voice was like her mother's, but with a fetching, exciting vibrato that hung on at the end of a word.

"What a nice doggie!" he heard the voice he was sure had to rival that of the angel's say, "Where did you come from?" and other pleasant chatter of delight as she greeted Nimrod. Tobias was near to shaking with apprehension and anxiety, desperation, almost, to see from what hallowed a creature such music could emanate.

"My God, Almighty, strengthen me," Tobias said silently, sending the prayer up to the throne where such desperate utterances are heard with a kindly ear.

"Father, there is the most wonderful doggie in here," she said stepping out into the courtyard. "Oh. I'm sorry, I've interrupted."

There she was. Nothing Azarias had said, nothing he had even hinted at, nothing he could have imagined could have prepared Tobias for that which was now before him.

"Ah, this is our daughter, Sarah," Raguel said. "Sarah, my dear, this is thy kinsman, Tobias, the son of my dear cousin, Tobit, the one who resides in Nineveh and about whom we spoke just the other night."

The girl nodded at Tobias, in the primal way of the young woman who sees one to her liking, and then to Azarias. She was far more beautiful than Azarias had indicated--far more beautiful than Tobias would have dared imagine. She stood in the reflected light, framed by two columns, illuminated and breathtaking. Her eyes, deep, deep brown, her nose, long and narrow, her cheeks (and the lad had no way of knowing this at the time, were flushed with excitement) had the glow of a light red wine, her brow, while showing traces of furrows from the sadness that had plagued her of late, was gentle, but strong. She held her magnificent, (her perfect, her glorious, and so on, as the

Tobias and the Angel

lad combed his vocabulary in search of words for an adequate description) head -- held it high, (bravely was what he saw). She was dressed in a simple, light blue drape, a golden sash about her narrow waist, and a gossamer veil, adorned with tiny, lovely, dark purple roses, accenting her face. The feeling rumbling through Tobias was not unlike the feeling of excitement before the fight yesterday -- frightening, yet compelling, exhilarating. Death, it quickly flitted through his mind, would not be too great a price for such a jewel. No. Not to have, to be near, not to live with this jewel, would be a sad and lonely death.

Azarias whispered to Tobias, "Is she all right?" Tobias couldn't answer. "I know how to pick 'em," Azarias continued while Tobias continued mute. "Well, say something. She'll think you're an idiot."

"Did you have a safe trip through the mountains?" The girl asked looking at both, but more at Azarias, averting looking directly at Tobias.

Clearing his throat, which had suddenly become filled with something, Tobias managed to say, feeling as he did so that he sounded like a boy whose voice was just changing: "It wasn't too bad. To save time, my friend Azarias, here, led us along the Old Smuggler's Road."

"I didn't know anyone still used that road," said Raguel.

"Not many do now. Azarias, here, is an experienced traveler and guide."

The girl spoke again: "I have heard it said that it is dangerous to traverse the mountains on any but the secure routes," she said, gaining in poise. Tobias couldn't bear to look directly at her, nor could he resist doing so, and so concentrating on his hands, he said, "That is true, I now know. But one can save often days in travel. And, Azarias is a skilled and competent guide. But, we did scare off a lion, and confront and defeat a gang of bandits."

"Bandits! How scary," she said, in admiration.

Azarias moved in on this: "Tobias didn't seem to think so, or he did a good job covering up his fears. I was afraid he was going to try and take on all five of them by himself."

Sarah looked at Tobias with a modest blush and genuine appreciation, then quickly looked back down and petted the dog.

Azarias went on, "and he is a fine fisherman, a good swordsman. And, Nimrod, here, (almost on cue the dog sat down in front of Sarah looking up at her adoringly, wagging his tail) did more than his share."

Sarah leaned over and put the adoring dog's head between her exquisite hands, "You mean he is a brave doggie as well as a handsome one?"

"Yes, indeed."

Raguel added, "Well, this is exciting and wonderful. But I am not being much of a host. Perhaps you will share all your adventures with us as you stay for dinner, and perhaps further honor us by spending the night?"

"That is certainly good of you. But Tobias is really in charge," Azarias, said, nodding to Tobias, with a stern look indicating what he was to say. Tobias coughed nervously, as he expressed thanks at the kind and generous offer.

"Edna, my dear, have the servants slaughter the finest, plumpest, blemish-free lamb in the flock. Have good Rebeccah work her greatest culinary magic. We must feast to celebrate the arrival of our fellow countrymen. Alleluia! Sarah, my dear, why don't you help your mother prepare for the feast?"

Sarah nodded her perfect head in acknowledgement, and turning to follow her mother, her eyes briefly caught Tobias' and she smiled at him. His heart stopped momentarily, and the poor lad was struck speechless. He was now hopelessly in love. Nimrod followed her out of the courtyard.

Tobias and the Angel

"Well, now, Jacob, we'll let the weary travelers freshen up and maybe get some rest before we feast in their honor. We have, of course, guestrooms, and one of the servants can lead you there. Azarias, is it? You needn't feel that you must leave first thing tomorrow. Please feel free to stay on several days, to get your strength up before going on to Rages."

Azarias said to Raguel, "Perhaps it would be best if the lad and I freshened up a bit. This has been his first time on the road, which can be a trying experience if you're not used to it. As you can see by the vacant expression on his face, he seems to be suffering the after effects of the journey now."

"Of course. He does seem a bit slow on the uptake, if you know what I mean," said the father of the most beautiful girl who had ever lived. Tobias, without saying a further word followed still another servant up toward the bathing area on the roof by the guests' quarters.

Entering the house Tobias passed a barely discernible figure in the shadows of the largest downstairs room. Doing so he felt a sudden chill, a sense that things were not quite right, and a quick shiver passed over, or through, him, as he walked by it. But once passed the presence, the ill feeling left him, and the little thought he gave it was only that perhaps he was both tired and hungry after his journey, and that he needed to acclimate himself to the altitude of Ecbatana.

An interminable hour or two passed before Azarias joined Tobias in the guest quarters. Together they walked out onto the roof, and looking out over the city, Tobias said, "Will you be doing the negotiating? I mean, asking Raguel to give me Sarah's hand as my bride? Or am I supposed to do it?"

"My, you've changed. Suddenly you're not so apprehensive? Ah, the ways of a lad with a maiden."

"Your idea of burning fish guts in the bridal chamber may not be so…"

"Just the fish heart -- not the entrails. I told you to throw away the entrails."

"'Guts' was just a figure of speech. Anyway, burning the heart on the coals may be a small price to pay. I'm still not so sure about the three nights of prayer, but I suppose if I am willing to go along with the fish heart, I mean ... well, I say my prayers every night anyway."

"I knew you'd see it my way."

"And, one more thing, Azarias: I don't think I want to wait till we come back from Rages."

"Toby, my boy, patience is the hardest at your age I know -- especially when it involves an affair of the heart. But..."

"It isn't just impatience, Azarias. I mean, suppose that, well,"

"No trust, huh?"

"It isn't that."

"You've actually thought this through, more or less."

"Can you help me secure the marriage commitment tonight -- I mean, if she'll have me -- Heavens, I didn't even think about that! What if she won't?"

"You'll worry yourself into an early grave."

"Thanks. That's just what I needed to hear."

"Metaphorically speaking. Didn't I tell you -- from before the world was made?"

"Right, that sounds good enough for me. Let's get on with it. Then if, well... those doubts again, sorry. You can always get my father's money, and ... you know."

"You're finally making good sense. I'll just check to see if the young lady will have you."

* * *

The young woman, it seems, was, in fact, just as smitten with Tobias as he was with her. But rather than finding the joy a

Tobias and the Angel

young heart normally finds in such an emotion, the poor girl and her mother were both unhappy about the situation. This was not for any wanting in Tobias, mind you; the girl just didn't want to lose "the best of the bunch" as she put it.

Old Raguel was also not overjoyed, but not because of Tobias; the boy seemed a father's dream of a son-in-law come true. The old man was concerned about the burial area behind their house. It was nearly full. Not to mention what this marriage, and the possible, if not probable, consequences might do to his cousin, Tobit.

Standing in the kitchen with her mother Sarah began to unburden her heart, "He is very handsome, this cousin of Papa's."

"Yes, he is. And he seems like such a good boy, too."

"If only..." the beautiful girl sighed.

Her mother sighed too. "Well, I don't believe that he is a suitor, my dear. At least there was nothing said about it before he came here, and nothing was said about it since he has been here. After all, they are on their way someplace else. But then he did look at you. And he is of the same tribe. He is well spoken, even if he doesn't seem real smart. And his father had been well off, and men like that usually regain their loss. God rewards the good, you know."

She sighed again. "I know," which seemed to indicate that she wasn't really convinced. And if it were so, what did that say about her?

"We will seek out the good God's will."

"I have, mother. But still ..."

* * *

Tobias and Azarias came into the dining room at the appointed time. The room was fragrant with roses and jasmine from the courtyard, just outside the room. Soft, golden light of the twilight came into the room with the fragrance of the flowers, and the lamps on stands about the room illuminated where the natural light failed, and compensated somewhat for the cool of the mountain evening.

Old Jacob was in the room waiting as they came in and made them welcome, chatting in small talk. Tobias leaned over to Azarias, and whispered, "When are you going to bring it up?"

"Bring what up?"

"Come on! You know ... When are you going to ask for Sarah's hand, for me? What's the matter, have you been drinking too much of his wine?"

"Relax. I don't drink."

Tobias lifted the goblet to his face, breathed in the rich bouquet, then took a deep swallow of the wine. It was delicious. He licked his lips.

Raguel came into the room and greeted his guests warmly. Then came Edna, who escorted the beautiful Sarah. She was clothed tonight in a soft gown of Indus silk, the color of wheat, with only a simple sash of blue on which was affixed a small corsage of gardenias. They stood together at the table and after a heart-felt prayer of thanksgiving, the roast lamb was brought to the table. A large bowl of salad greens garnished with chives, sliced truffles, coated with honey, vinegar and olive oil, was brought out, and another bowl of onion-flavored kashi. There was too, another large jar of a young, light-bodied, semi-sweet red wine. Everyone ate in silence, savoring the goodness of the meal. Tobias kept sneaking glances at the girl, who kept her wonderful eyes down in apparent rapt attention to the plate before her. She seemed to be spending more time studying the wonders on her plate than eating them. It crossed Tobias' mind that perhaps he was not to the girl's liking. And the best that could be hoped for was a traditional arranged marriage, one that would make the three nights of prayer only too acceptable -- at least to her. He also kept glancing to the other side to see when

Tobias and the Angel

Azarias was going to say something. Everyone just kept munching away. Finally the silence was broken when Raguel said, "Our Rebeccah is certainly the best cook in the city."

It was an opening for Tobias to talk about something: "We also have a serving girl called Rebeccah. She is a young girl, and very competent."

Sarah glanced up him, then back down at her plate immediately. It quickly zipped through her mind that with a young girl in his house, Tobias had probably already tasted of the flesh, and with a girl in the house at his beck and call, he would be in no hurry to marry. Her heart began to sink. She fought any show, and continued to pick at her plate.

Azarias caught the brief, slight change of expression on the girl's face and chose that moment to speak to Raguel, "Raguel, you know of course, that your beautiful daughter, Sarah, is eligible, indeed obligated, to one of her own tribe."

The older gentleman cleared his throat, and after a pause, said, "Yes, we have been quite aware of that. But, young men of her own tribe are not that easy to find."

Under his breath Tobias whisper to Azarias, "Probably none left--at least in these parts."

Azarias kicked Tobias under the table and said under his breath: "Quiet. You want them to hear you?" (Then back to Raguel): "Our clansman, Tobias here, finds your daughter...

(Again, Tobias said under his breath) "Gorgeous" -- (and) "Ouch!" (To the elbow in his ribs) "... but Dangerous!" And "Ouch!" Again to another kick at his shins.

Azarias added under his breath, "Leave the wine alone if you can't handle it any better than that, you jerk." Azarias continued to Raguel, "Tobias is, it seems, drawn to your daughter as Isaac was to Rebecca. And has asked me to present to you the fact that he would be honored if you would honor him and his parents with the promise of her hand -- providing, of course, that the young lady finds him acceptable."

Raguel cleared his throat again, and with an even expression said, "Well, of course. I'm sure she does?" Her father looked over at the maiden sitting quietly, and with an inscrutable expression on her face. Her father went on, "I'm sure too there is no one but himself who should have our daughter Sarah." He smiled, cautiously, and looked over at her.

Under his breath again, Tobias said to Azarias: "Small wonder, every one else is dead."

"Will you cut that out?" Azarias said as he shot the tipsy lad a withering look.

Raguel continued, "Indeed I have no right to give her to anyone else, since you, Tobias, are my nearest kinsman -- after, of course, your father. But I must tell you the truth, my son:"

Sarah interrupted, her head up now and looking directly at her father: "Father, please! Let us not go into the details. It would be better if Tobias were to…"

"Please, my daughter, the truth must always be told in such a situation."

"I'm all too painfully aware of that, Father."

Raguel went on, "I have given her in marriage to seven of our kinsmen and, ah, well, you may have heard, they all died on their wedding night."

"Whew! Nothing like getting it out into the open." Tobias said softly to Azarias -- and which the girl didn't hear because at her father's words she rose majestically, magnificently, beautifully, Tobias thought, looking over at her. He rose too, and stood gaping as she left the room and went out into the courtyard alone, leaving behind a scent as delicate as a moonflower. An older woman, Rebeccah, had entered the room, and now followed the girl. It was apparent this woman, Rebeccah, the cook, was also probably something of an auxiliary mother. She was rushing off to comfort Sarah, while her mother, Edna, remained at the table, tears glistening in the corner of her eyes.

Tobias and the Angel

"Please," Raguel went on, "forgive the girl. She is not often given to outbursts. A more even-tempered, gentle girl doesn't exist. But the burden she has born these past years is beginning to take its toll." The older gentleman sighed. He went on after another pause, "And there is this: my kinsman, Tobit, also has had more than his share of troubles. If the two were to be married and the same fate awaited the lad here ... well, I would hate to bear the knowledge that I had contributed to his father's suffering."

"To say nothing of mine," Tobias added, with a brief hiccough, "and my poor, dear mother's."

"You may rest assured, my good friend," Azarias said simply and firmly, "for I have it on the highest authority that the will of the Almighty is for these two to be joined."

Raguel looked at Azarias' face, which had about it that look it sometimes got when he was uttering an irrefutable statement. No one who saw this facial expression could or would question it. Raguel's own face broke into a broad, happy smile, as he said, "Well, then, my son, eat now and drink, and may the Lord, our God, deal kindly with you both," and with that he raised a goblet of freshly poured wine and, toasting the couple, drank deeply.

Tobias, who was still standing, although waving slightly, said, "Sir, your answer 'srather indefinite. Could you be more sfecisific?" he managed to slur out.

"I'm not sure what you want me to say?" The older man said, looking questioningly at the lad.

"We 'ere talking about your daughter, sir -- Well, I cannot eat, or even drink, anything here until we have disposed of this business of mine."

Azarias, understood what the young man was trying to say, "Sir, the young fellow is studying the craft of the scribe, which means also that of law -- he's a natural nitpicker. What he seeks is a definite commitment of the hand of your daughter Sarah in marriage--to him." (And to Tobias he said:) "That is what you're getting at, right?" Tobias nodded, and even grinned.

Azarias continued: "Do not be afraid to give him, normally a rather sober young man, thy daughter's hand; for to his care she was destined, that is why those other wooers could not, shall we say, gain their suit."

"Oh yes, yes -- of course. Very well, then: Yes! It is done! The girl is yours, my lad!"

And Tobias sank into his chair, raised his goblet first to Raguel, then Edna, then Azarias, then to his mouth and drank deeply.

Raguel went on with tears of joy streaking his fine old face: "All those prayers and sighs of mine were not wasted; God has granted them audience; and I doubt not that his design in bringing you here was to have my daughter matched with one of her own kin, as the law of Moses bade. Heaven has ordained that she shall be yours. From now on you belong to her and she to you; she is yours forever from this day. Alleluia! The Lord of heaven prosper you both this night, my son, and grant you mercy and peace! Edna, my dear, please bring the young woman back in!"

Rebeccah, the auxiliary mother, who must have been listening by the door, wasted no time in fetching the girl, and pulling her by her thin, delicate, beautiful arm, brought her back into the dining room.

Raguel stood and went and gently taking his daughter's arm tenderly, kissed her on her tear-streaked cheek. Then he gently nudged her toward Tobias, saying: "Take her, my son, to be your wedded wife; take her home to your Father; and may the God of Abraham, Isaac and Jacob, be with you and himself join you in one, and fulfill his merciful purpose in you. And give you peace and prosperity. Amen! Alleluia!"

Sarah looked up into Tobias' eyes, and he sank into hers. She extended her hands to him, and he took them into his own.

Tobias and the Angel

They were warm, smooth, soft, and alive with all the force of life and love that pulsates from the hands of a virgin. Tears touched the corner of the lad's eyes as he looked into the eyes of his beloved. All he could manage to say was "Wow!"

"Edna, my dear, prepare me the paper that I may write out a marriage contract granting Sarah to Tobias as his wife, as the law of Moses ordains, and the terms of her dowry."

And in an almost giddy mood, but still not without a certain apprehension, the papers are signed, the vows exchanged, and the marriage became at that moment, a legal fact. Everyone, including the servants, mother and father, the young folks, even Azarias, gathered again at the table to witness the signing of the contract. Then they all ate and drank; until at last Raguel said to his wife, "My dear, have the servants prepare the spare room, make it ready, for the young ones, then you take our daughter to prepare her to receive her new husband."

Robert Wanless

Chapter 12
The Wedding Night In the bridal chamber

The "bridal chamber" was actually the room wherein we first met Sarah and in which she had contemplated suicide. And, too, it is where the sad girl had finally prayed that heartfelt prayer. You may remember that the room had, in fact, been referred to for many years as the Bridal chamber more often than as the "spare room", at least by the women in the house.

Edna and Rebeccah had set the room up as such first when Sarah had become a young woman. Over the years the three women had worked on it, elegantly and lovingly decorating it. It had become increasingly Sarah's private place. The seven times it had served as the place of, if not tragedy, certainly sadness, didn't dispel the hope that filled the two, Edna and Sarah, mother and daughter, as they entered the room together again this night. And while hope glowed in the souls of each woman, they were both nevertheless, apprehensive. Sarah tried to lessen the tension as they entered quipping: "We're getting pretty good at doing this, aren't we, Mother? I suppose, sooner or later, I'll get it right?"

Edna said nothing as she went to the wardrobe and removed the bridal nightgown. She checked it out, pulling at a loose thread, smoothing it with her hands, all the while saying nothing and trying her best not to look sad or nervous. Sarah looked at the gown. It was a new one, one she had never worn, made after the last sad betrothal. Her mother had made it in an attempt not to lose heart. The girl took a deep breath, then sighed. The sigh wasn't one of sadness, but more like a deep breath before beginning something one knew would take some exertion. In truth she did feel more hopeful--far more, in fact, than she had felt in quite some time--but still a little afraid.

Her mind wandered back, briefly, to the mornings she had awakened to find the corpse of her betrothed lying next to her, sleep having overtaken her in the night as death had overtaken the young man. She pushed these thoughts away, after she recalled one, an older distant cousin, terribly overweight, and foul smelling. He certainly hadn't been a *young man*. She felt a tinge of guilt when she admitted to herself that maybe his "untimely death" wasn't the saddest of the seven she had had to endure. Then for just an instant, she recalled the beast and her challenge to him that fateful day not so long ago. She had never really seen him, or it, before, only known his presence. That last time, that day when she had prayed so, there was desperation about him. It was the first she had heard him clearly, and nearly seen him, or it. She shook her pretty head to rid her mind of any further such thoughts. She looked at the bridal nightgown and shrugged, then forced a smile.

It was Edna's turn now to try a little levity: "Well, my dearest one, let's see if it still fits."

Sarah removed her evening dress, and stood nearly naked before her mother. Her mother looked at the beautiful creature she had born, nursed and loved and with, and for whom, she had wept, these last few years.

She smiled at the dear, lovely face. She had an elongated oval head and almond shaped eyes, too large perhaps, or seeming so because of the deepness of their brown color. The eyes were beneath a brow now slightly furrowed, and sloping down to the center, her long slender, delicate and aristocratic nose. Her mouth was a deep red, of a hue similar to the roses in her veil, and which her father tended so carefully. She had never the need to add any rouge to redden it. It was turned down slightly now, sad like. She was a tall girl, and ripe now in the full flowering of her young womanhood. Shapely too, her shoulders, though somewhat broad, curved gently down from her long and graceful neck, rounding out for her chest. Her

Tobias and the Angel

breasts resembled small pink pomegranates, (or so Sarah thought looking at herself in the mirror) and from which soon, surely, a husky baby would drink. Down now, her mother looked, from her narrow waist to her little tummy ever so slightly enlarged. Her long thighs and calves, gently formed pillars, smooth, creamy and downy, stretching down from her light brown, crisp, hair coated triangle in the temple of her smoothly rounded hips. Her mother sighed now, reflecting on the exquisite virginal beauty, the fresh glow of youth of this her only child, her beloved daughter. "Here my lovely one, let's clothe your beauty in this holy frock. And, God willing, you will soon be filled with the love of your husband." And she touched her dear face. "You are warm?"

"Yes, mother."

"Are you wet too?"

"Yes mother."

"Ahhhh. God willing this time next year you'll be nursing and loving your own babe."

"Yes, mother," the girl whispered blushing, and tears welling up in her lovely eyes.

As her mother draped the robe over her head, Sarah, with a tear in her voice said, "He is handsome, isn't he, mother."

"He is very handsome, my dear."

"You know, I think he is the best of them. At least I like him the best of all," and saying this she began to weep.

"Now, now, my dear. Don't you start weeping, or I'm sure to join you. Yes, he is handsome. I think I like him the best too. And he seems like such a good boy, too; so respectful of his parents." And with that Edna also broke into sobs. The two women embraced and wept quietly in each other's arms for a time.

"There now, enough of this! Don't lose heart, dear; thou hast had sadness enough. May the Lord of Heaven give thee gladness in exchange. Buck up, my dear. Courage now, courage! Prepare yourself. You are very beautiful. And that other fellow, the young man's guide, he seems very -- well, he seems different, I guess, but so authoritative. He has said to thy father he has it on the highest authority that everything will be all right -- hum?"

"Yes, mother. I'm fine, now -- I think."

Edna then went to the bed and smoothed it down, moving the coverlet off the pillows, but not actually turning the bed down for the night. That might embarrass the couple. She went then to the windows, and leaving them open for the cool but fragrant mountain breezes to enter, she drew the sheer curtains over the opening. She went over to the brazier Jacob had left for warmth and fragrance. In it was a plate of hot coals. She stirred the coals with the poker. "I'll leave the lamps burning." Again she looked at her daughter. "I'll leave you alone, now." And hugging the girl once more, kissing her sweetly on the smooth and glowing cheek, the mother left the bridal chamber, with a quivering chin and a stifled sob, leaving her beloved daughter alone.

Sarah stood in silence. When she could no longer hear her mother steps down the hall, she began to look around the room. She took a sniff here and there, walked over near the bed and did the same, then by the wardrobe, then to the windows. She quickly knelt down and looked under the bed. Satisfied she stood again. While she felt a certain apprehension, she also began to feel resolve. She was not going to lose this betrothed. It was not so much that she might not get another, it was that she felt so much more for him. He was young, tall, and really, rather handsome. Resolved then to do whatever might be necessary, she raised her eyes up to heaven, but could find no words to utter in prayer, she simply sighed again, then nodded. Almost on cue, there was a knock at the door. Nervously she walked over and opened it.

Tobias and the Angel

It was Tobias. He too was nervous. She stepped aside, as he walked into the room and stood in front of her. He closed the door, gently, quietly. They looked at each other and smiled shyly. He was wearing a white tunic, trimmed in gold thread. He had washed his face, and combed his hair, stained a light copper-like color, from the past several days in the sun. His face was tanned and she thought, looking at him, that he was the most marvelous creature she had ever seen. He greeted his new bride by extending his hands out to her, and they joined hands briefly. He could think of nothing to say. His handsome face and the way he looked at her with adoring eyes seemed to say all she would ever want to hear. She couldn't stop her mouth from dropping open.

He squeezed her hands gently, then released them and walked over to the brazier, which stood, on a small heavy metal stand against the back wall. He had worn a hip wallet, around to his backside. He removed this and took out the fish heart, dry now after several days being rolled in salt and wrapped up in palmetto fronds. He placed the heart on the coals and watched as it began to burn and give off smoke. The smoke was white and fragrant, not all together too 'fishy" a fragrance, more like creosote, or tar. The fragrance began to spread throughout the room visibly from the acrid smoke. Sarah looked on in silence and with a growing trust in the young man before her. She smelled the fragrance and said, "Dearest husband, pray, what is that incense you've put on the brazier?"

"It isn't incense, my bride; it is a fish heart."

"Oh," she replied, not wanting to seem stupid, almost as if she had heard of fish heart used on wedding nights in the past, but having never actually met a bridegroom with the good sense to use it. So she went on, "fish heart! The fragrance is certainly unusual -- very pungent. Joshiel, he was the third, I think, burned a mixture of pine and cinnamon as incense -- or was he the fourth?"

145

Tobias said nothing. In truth he wasn't sure now how he was to do the things Azarias had told him to do -- even though Azarias had reminded him after dinner, but without much specificity. For instance, was he supposed to wait until the fish-heart was consumed in the flames before he started praying? Then, was he supposed to hold her hands as they prayed? Were they to stand facing each other; or side by side facing the east, or west to the Holy Land that had been promised to their forefathers? He finally uttered a prayer, silently, for God to guide him. He jumped, literally, at a sudden flash of lightening, followed instantly by loud crash of thunder. If this was God talking to him, he thought, he didn't understand what the Almighty had said -- but it sure got his attention.

"Whew!" he said looking over to Sarah, "do you get summer storms up in these parts?"

"In the afternoons, not usually at night," she answered.

A sudden breeze blew in and disturbed the window curtains. He decided to overlook the weather outside and go on explaining what he, they, were going to have to do. "My friend, Azarias, who is knowledgeable in the ways of, well, in all sorts of ways, has instructed me in what we (he paused at the plural, then went on), what we are supposed to do this evening."

"Oh?" the tender beauty said, looking with a mixture of trust and curiosity at her young man. Her attention drifted off as she thought about how he seemed much taller now and seemed broader across the chest, and so much stronger looking, now that they were close.

Meanwhile, the thunder and lightening continued outside, building in intensity. The breeze had turned to a full-fledged wind now, and the curtains were billowing in, almost filling the room, like taunting, daring even, specters.

"Azarias has his peculiarities," Tobias went on, acting oblivious to the goings on, "but his heart is in the right place. He is very wise, intelligent and good fun. He seems to have

Tobias and the Angel

traveled all over the world." Tobias paused again, looking at the curtains nervously, then went on, "Now, my love, let us hold hands; and together beseech our Lord, as Azarias has instructed me, to show us his mercy and keep us safe -- tonight." he added with a swallow.

The girl's faith in her new husband strengthened and she moved closer to him, reaching out and taking his hands in hers. The thunder and lightening continued to intensify outside, and the curtains waved in the breeze within the room. Tobias began to pray aloud, saying the words as they came to him:

"We praise thee, O God of our fathers, forever and ever.
Let the heavens and all thy creation praise thee forever."

The smoke rising from the fish heart on the brazier became denser; filling the room, swirling in the wind which now blew fiercely in the window and now blew out one of the lamps.

"Uh oh, I've seen this before," Sarah said interrupting Tobias. And she held his hands tighter in growing terror. "Oh no. On no!" she said, with a note of anger in her voice. The wind became more intense and another lamp blew out.

Tobias also became frightened, but his fear soon turned to anger. He tried to pose strong and resolute, saying to Sarah, "Be strong, my bride."

"Oh, no oh no, oh no! Please! Please! NO!" The girl said, and while there was still anger, there was also more fear. She let go of his hands and covered her beautiful face with her long hands. Tobias seeing the face he loved beyond anything he had ever seen, stuck with horror, he became determined to match this occasion. He felt himself almost swelling up, as the room became nearly dark.

Tobias rushed over to the window to close the shutters, at least to stop the wind, and probably the rain, if and when it started. But when he pushed the curtains back out of the way, a dark being lunged in through the window and knocked him down. The demon emitted a shrill whistling sound that filled the room. Tobias struggled to get to his feet. He tried to discern the being in the dimly lighted room, and, meanwhile, continued his praying:

"We praise thee, O God of our fathers, forever and ever.
Let the heavens and all thy creation praise thee forever.
Thou madest Adam, then said
it is not good for the man to be alone;
let us make him a helper like himself."

At this the being reached out for Tobias, putting his cold, damp hands, or tentacles, around the young man's neck. Tobias suddenly felt anger at what was happening, then a surge of strength. He brought his own two hands together, and quickly up in front of him, breaking the demon's grip.

"You son-of-a-bitch!" Tobias said aloud, "I'm not going to roll over and die like those others. You want to kill me you're going to have to work at it." And he jumped back into a wrestler's stance.

Sarah heard Tobias' words and saw him move to fight the beast. She moved quickly out of the way, and looked around for something she could swing at the beast. But the beast suspected as much and swelled up, growing to twice his size, in front of the girl, then let out a hideous hissing shriek. Sarah was caught off guard by the intensity of hatred directed at her, and fell back onto the bed in utter horror.

"Leave her alone, you stinking coward. You want to mess with someone; I'm the one."

The beast tried the same routine on Tobias, a greenish glowing swelling presence of intense hatred, a huge foul-smelling presence filling the space directly in front of Tobias. It almost did the trick. Tobias stunned by the intensity of the evil immediately before him, staggered back, unable immediately to

Tobias and the Angel

gain control of himself. The beast was about to jump on Tobias with the most deadly, fierce, demented look on his hideous face, plainly ready to finish off this young man as he had the rest, but with a vengeance; none of the others had dared to offer anywhere near this much resistance. But his attempt was thwarted.

Suddenly there was another loud crash of thunder and the door to the room burst open--just as Tobias fell back on the floor. Standing before him now was none other than the great archangel, St. Raphael himself; standing there in a shimmering golden glow of strength and of divine power. Tobias, with his eyes wide open in awe, got to his feet again. Now there were three in the melee, at least briefly.

"Azarias, is that you?" Tobias asked, before being knocked to the floor again. And this time he hit his head against one of the metal legs of the brazier and was knocked out.

Sarah, who had been watching all of this stunned in frozen terror, found strength to move and jumped to aid her beloved. She threw herself over him, covering him, while the other two kept at it, knocking things over, slugging, swirling, turning, in a dance of transcendent proportions, import and intensity. The battle became ever more fierce, with each of the ancient cousins straining, as once such combatants did in that time before time, before the world began, and as they will again, at that future time, when good and evil fight their final round. Raphael, the archangel, then, with a sudden, swift, and decisive blow, subdued Asmodeaus. And there was stillness, quiet. The storm outside, as the one within, passed.

It was Azarias; now, who rose and began to bind his ancient foe tightly with a rope he had brought with him. He moved quickly, binding up tightly and completely the figure, which had become again an amorphous difficult-to-distinguish figure, a crumpled mass upon the floor. He lay now defeated and humiliated in the bridal chamber where he had known seven victories. There was total silence now.

After what seemed ages to Sarah, still in frozen silence, but fully conscious of what had been going on, the demon found his voice again: "Come on, Raphey, old boy, have a heart. You've won this one. Now let me go. You're hurting me."

"Awww! You're breaking my heart. You always were a whiner," said Azarias.

"Look, let me go and I promise I'll never bother the girl again -- honest."

"Honest! Did you say HONEST? Why, Assiness...

"That's ASMODEAUS!"

"Whatever. Asmodeaus, you said 'Honest.' Why, if you told the truth, you wouldn't be you, now, would you?"

The demon seemed to think about that for a few moments, then said; "how am I supposed to answer that?"

"You're finished here."

"Ah ha. See how you talk. Where is your charity, huh? And you call yourself one of *His*! You're no better than -- You're just a hypocrite!"

"I know. You just don't get no respect, do you?" Then to Tobias he said, "Hey, Toby! Toby! Come on, get up and give me a hand. I need you to open the door for me?"

The lovely Sarah eased up and could scarcely look at Azarias. She leaned back down and gently kissed Tobias on the forehead, gently speaking his name. It took Tobias a few moments to come to. It was quiet in the room now, but he did recognize Azarias. He got up off the floor, rubbing the knot on his head, and cautiously limped over to the door and opened it. Azarias nodded over to Sarah, still sitting on the floor. Azarias smiled at him, and gave the "OK" sign with his hands. He said, "See you later," and he dragged the dark figure out of the room. Tobias closed the door. The room was so quiet he was sure his bride would hear his heart still pounding. He tried, but only for

Tobias and the Angel

a moment, to consider all that had happened. What had he seen? Who, and more importantly, what was that creature that Azarias had beaten and dragged out of the room? But just as quickly these thoughts vanished from his mind as he saw his beautiful bride sitting now on the bed. Suddenly his whole body throbbed with life, as he looked at her sitting on the bed and looking at him what had to be adoringly. Then, just as suddenly, thoughts of the agreement made with Azarias, especially in the light of the activities in this room, made him say to his bride, "My dearest. Get up, my love, my dove, my tender one."

Sarah stood up and looked around at the mess the room was in, which she could see now since moonlight filled the room illuminating what the one remaining lamp didn't.

"Did he do it? I mean, did you help him drive out the demon?"

"Well, yes, I suppose I did help a little. But the truth is that my friend, Azarias, came in and finished the job. I'm afraid that I got knocked out."

"But, you stood up to him!"

"I guess I did. Anyway, I don't think we'll have any more to fear from that demon. Come then, my beloved, let us again begin to pray. We must first of all thank our God for delivering us, and beseech him to show us mercy and keep us safe. Where was I?"

"I think you had started talking about Eve?"

"Right ...

Thou madest Eve his wife, to be his helper and support;
and these two were the parents of the human race.
I now take this, my beloved to be my wife,
not out of lust but in true marriage.
Grant that she and I may find mercy and grow old together."

And they both said 'Amen'

Then Sarah added her own prayer:

*"Thank you Lord for having heard my prayers and rescued us.
Have mercy on us, Lord, have mercy on us;
keep us safe from all harm as we grow old together, he and I."*

And Tobias said, "Now my dearest one, let us go to sleep."

"To sleep?" the beautiful, doe eyed maiden said to her husband.

"Yes, dearest, tonight, tomorrow, and the day after, we must pray God for mercy. Tomorrow we are to pray for the blessing of children ..."

"There is another way to get the blessing of children, Toby, dear."

"I know, but ... Azarias said, it was part of the deal -- well, I promised Azarias that these three nights would be set apart for our union with God; then, when the third is over, we will be joined as one, thou and I. He has reminded me that we come of holy lineage. We are not to mate blindly, like the heathen that have no knowledge of God. And in view of what Azarias did for us tonight, I think maybe we'd better keep our word."

The maiden looked at her new husband, thought briefly about all that she had seen this night, and with the gentlest, the most subtle of shrugs, she replied: "You're right."

Chapter 13

Out in Raguel's backyard the next morning

Early the next morning, in the pale predawn light, two men walked out of Raguel's house to the back wall of the property. The men carried implements for digging. Over one's shoulder, was a pick, over the other, two spades. The two men walked rather in the easy march of soldiers, chatting together as old friends on their way to fish in a friendly old spot. The two men, of course, were Raguel and his servant, old Jacob. They were on their way to begin digging another grave, while their neighbors were still asleep. It had become an unfortunate routine of the morning following Sarah's seven previous wedding nights. There was little reason to change the routine on this, the eighth.

Old Jacob had spoken first, breaking the predawn silence: "With all that storming last night you'd think the ground would be too wet to dig."

"Yes, but it doesn't appear to have rained at all," Raguel answered. "Which is just as well. This grave digging is hard enough on my tired old bones, without the added weight of wet ground."

The two men continued walking until they reached the back wall. Stopping, Raguel said, as he sized up the area for digging, "I'm sure this will be the last one. Let's dig this grave over there near the end of the wall. With any luck we can lay the young fellow out before any of the neighbors awake."

"It is embarrassing, isn't it, sir?" said his friend and servant.

"Aye, embarrassing and tiring."

"Well, let me do the digging, sir. You shouldn't have to exert yourself. You've troubles enough wearing you down without the planting of still another -- Anyway; I've strength enough for us both."

"Now, what are you saying, old friend, you're stronger than the both of us? Jacob, you seem to forget you're much older than I am"

"I'm not meaning to slight you, sir. But I've not enjoyed having my strength sapped by wealth and servants."

"Ha! Well, you've had a job all these years haven't you? And judging by looks of you, hunger hasn't been one of your great problems -- nor overwork either."

"That it hasn't sir, and thankful for it I am. And I count it a blessing to have been in your service all this time."

"And it has been as much as a friend as a servant."

"Aye, and you as much a friend as a master, yourself."

The two old friends, master and servant, continued chatting as they did most days: "Let's see now, this would be number eight, wouldn't it?" the servant added.

"Eight it is."

"I do hope this is the last one, we're surely running out of room," said Jacob. Raguel nodded sadly. "Sorry, sir, I was just trying to make light of a heavy situation. I know it's a heavy burden on you and the missus -- to say nothing of the young lady."

Old Jacob paced out an area three feet from the wall, then walked another six feet on, and with another foot for good measure. He marked one corner, measured two feet across, and then sank his spade into the ground. Raguel joined him at the head of the gravesite, and he too began to dig. "I'll give you some help, anyway."

"Be easy about it. I don't want to have to do number nine alone, if you know what I mean." Each man took a good spade full and tossed it to the side.

Raguel paused after a few spade fulls and said: "I hope there won't be a lot of trouble over this one, the missus gets so upset, and the young lady too ... not to mention the officials, what with the neighbors commenting and all."

Tobias and the Angel

Like municipal workers, both men would take a few spadefuls of dirt, and stop to talk, then dig again. Old Jacob stopped, and seemed touched as he said, "This one seemed a lot different from the others, I thought."

"I did too, and what's sad is, so did the daughter. He was a handsome, decent boy, not like one of those other yard cocks, strutting, and primping."

"Maybe that's what did them yard cocks in, getting their necks strangled in something too small for them?"

"No. The girl's still inviolate, says her dam. She's a dainty lass."

Old Jacob, stopping again and resting on the spade said, "On first seeing the lad, I says to myself, 'Now this is a happy meeting'."

"I said the same -- to myself."

"And the tall one, the guide, he calls himself, there's a strange one for you. There was something about him, some energy, almost like a glow, or so it seemed."

Raguel said, slowing again on the digging. "Now that you mention it, I thought I saw it too. But I thought it was the light playing off the house across the way." His friend and servant agreed, and began to take up the slack, saying, "but my eyes are not as bright as once they were, so I'm likely off the mark with that one."

The two worked together in silence for a time. Both men stopped and straightened up, stretching. Raguel looked toward the house and saw Edna and Kashima coming toward them carrying a jar of steaming tea and drinking bowls. "Here comes refreshment."

"And just in time."

"We'll refresh the old mules," Raguel said patting his own chest and nodding toward Jacob, "Then I'll have the maid go up and check on the Daughter. We should be ready then to bring the poor fellow down and lay him to rest, before it gets much lighter out."

Edna and the maid arrived and handed each man his morning tea, which they drank heartily. "Edna, my dear, have Kashima go upstairs and see if it is alright to bring the body down."

"Raggy, my dear, Kashi has expressed her reluctance to enter that chamber again."

"It's nothing she hasn't seen before. I know she and Sarah have not been getting on well. That's the real reason. She can do as she's told."

Flicking her eyebrows up, in acquiescence, Edna said to the girl "Kashi, my dear, please go upstairs and rouse Sarah. Tell her we have to bring down the young man to bury before it's light. Away with you now."

"I don't like doing this, ma'am. I feel like I'm part of some kind of wrongdoing -- 'conspirry'-- I s'pose they call it."

"Nonsense. There's no conspiracy, as you call it. We're not the ones doing in the lads, nor is it Sarah. Now be on your way. We'll have some nice hot tea and sweet cakes inside when we're done."

Jacob handed his bowl to Edna, wiped his mouth with his sleeve, thanked her and began digging again

"I think that is deep enough, Old friend," Raguel said to his servant.

Jacob nodded in agreement, "Aye, sir, so it seems and so my back tells me." They were standing now nearly chest high in the grave. With some effort Jacob climbed out of the grave first then extended his hand to assist Raguel.

Edna watched the two old men, then looked over to the eastern mountains. She said, "Everything seems different this time, Raggy. Did you notice?"

Tobias and the Angel

"Well, I admit that guide fellow seemed to speak with a great deal of authority. But then there was that stormin' last night. I thought we were going to have an earthquake."

"I didn't hear anything."

"You slept through it all?"

"I must have. I thought I heard some rumpus upstairs, but I closed my ears to it, what with the young folks and all ..."

"We'll get this business over with then. Now, I've given some thought, to, perhaps, sending the girl to Nineveh for a while, perhaps to help my cousin Tobit, and his wife, with their difficulties. I'm sure she won't want to stay around here."

"Oh, no! good husband, don't send my darling girl away!"

"Well, not forever, my dear, but for a time to help those people over their grief, and get the girl away from gossip."

Their conversation was interrupted with Kashima running, excitedly, back to join them, barely able to speak, but managing to blurt out, as she stumbled to a stop before Edna, "He ain't dead, ma'am."

Edna replied, "Not dead? Oh surely you're mistaken?"

Raguel, inclined to be impatient with the girl, snapped, "Now, don't be silly, girl. Get back up there and tell Sarah to get up, we've burying to do. Go on with you now ..."

"Missus, please tell your husband I ain't being silly. I looked in the room and they was both asleep -- fully clothed, they was, and laying on top of the bed covers. But they was asleep. She was cuddled up close to him, his arm was around her shoulder, but he was asleep, and not dead ... and they had their clothes all on!"

Raguel's impatience seemed to take on a slight note of hopefulness. "Now, Edna, how could that girl tell if the lad was asleep and not dead?"

"Ma'am, tell your husband that I knows the difference betwixt someone sleeping and someone dead. Anyway, I touched him and he moved," and she blushed and put her head down and giggled, then added emphatically, "he ain't dead."

It was starting to sink in. Edna smiled and said, "You don't say?" Her face was beginning to glow with hope.

"I do say, ma'am. Please come up with me and see for yourself. And furthermore, the room's one awful mess, like they been fighting all the night and just dropped down to sleep. I've never lied to you or your husband."

"These young people today! Let me go see." And Edna rushed off to see for herself.

"I hope you're not making a mistake, girl," Raguel said sternly to the girl. "This kind of foolishness would break my dear wife's heart. What do you say, old friend? Shall we go see what all's about?"

"I'd not miss it, even if I had to get out of my own grave to see," said Old Jacob, and the two men followed Edna. The girl picked up the jar and two bowls off the ground and followed the men, mumbling about no one believing her.

When the men got to the house and entered the courtyard through the rear entrance they were met by Edna who had rushed back down to tell the men what she had seen. Delighted, she said, "Husband, the girl is right, the room's one awful mess, but they are both still alive. I don't know what on earth they were doing in there last night to make all that mess -- and them still fully clothed and all." She stopped and looked at her husband, her blush suddenly turned to a look approaching horror, contorting the normally placid brow, "Oh no," she said. "Maybe they just didn't hit it off."

Tobias and Sarah entered the courtyard just then, holding hands, smiling and saying with voices filled with happy, youthful buoyancy: "Good Morning, everybody."

And everybody acknowledged that it was in fact a very good morning.

Tobias and the Angel

* * *

It was later that same day that Azarias returned to Raguel's house and greeted the family. As Raphael he had taken the demon, Asmodeaus, bound tightly, all the way to Egypt, traveling the way to which he was most accustomed. There he dropped the beast, and there the beast remains. Tobias greeted his friend and guide warmly, still excited, almost too much so to talk. He excused himself and Azarias from the others and together the two walked out into the garden.

"Toby, my friend, you look none the worse for wear. How's your head?"

"It still hurts a little, but I feel wonderful. Azarias, my friend, I am simply unable to thank you or make any return for all you have given me, for all thy watchful care of me, even if I should offer myself to be thy slave. My heart is so full. But instead of that, here I am asking of thee one more favor. Could you, would you, go on to Rages, give Gabelus back his bond, recover the money, and bring it back. Then we can be on our way to Nineveh."

"And what are you going to do when I'm away?" Azarias asked, teasing.

"Why? Do you think that slime-bucket who was here last night will come back?"

"Hardly."

"Well. there is this too. Raguel has pleaded with me to stay on. And well, the girl, my wife, -- It sounds funny to say that, 'my wife' -- doesn't seem to want me out of her sight, and -- well, she -- I don't want to give them the impression..."

"Well, I'll tell you, I had planned to go on my own. You may recall, unless your head suffered more than we realized at first, that we talked about just this thing. I'll do it, and I should be back in two days."

"Azarias, there is no way you can go all the way to Rages and back in two days."

"How do you know?"

"Common sense."

"What one needs to do the impossible is uncommon sense."

Raguel came out and joined the two standing and discussing the above, and asked the nature of the talk.

Tobias told him: "I am sending Azarias on to Rages to collect my father's bond."

"Ah, good. Then you will stay here while he is doing your errand, and protect your bride. Good. And, my friend," he addressed the following to Azarias: "there is so much that I owe you for bringing this remarkable young man to survive being wed to my daughter. For that I feel I must return something to you. Jacob, come here! Arrange a train for our friend, Azarias, here. Four camels, and aids to lead and comfort and serve him on his way to Rages."

"Raguel, my good man," Azarias interrupted, "I can make much better time..."

"Of course you can. But I want you to bring Gabelus and his family back with you to help in the celebration of my daughter's wedding."

The jubilant old man was too much even for Azarias. The guide agreed. Azarias went with the four servants and the camels to Rages in Media and gathered Gabelus and his family for the return trip. It was as a successful businessman, that Gabelus returned Tobit's bond, with interest, and thanks, counting out the bags to Azarias with their seals intact. Tobit's money had ended up being used for security on a short-term high interest demand note. Gabelus repaid the note in time and not being able readily to get in touch with Tobit, he reinvested the money at rates just this side of usury, and made even more money. So it was a handsome sum indeed that was returned to Tobit.

Tobias and the Angel

Azarias informed Gabelus that Tobit's son, Tobias, had taken a wife in Ecbatana, none other than the daughter of Raguel. The man stared at Azarias dumbstruck. Then when he extended the invitation to the wedding-feast, he replied, "The boy married that girl -- and has lived to tell about it? I'll go to that wedding feast, I will."

The next morning Gabelus and his family, all made an early start, and in a remarkably short time returned to Ecbatana and the wedding feast. When they arrived in Ecbatana, and entered Raguel's house, Gabelus found Tobias and ran over to him, with tears in his eyes, he blessed the boy saying:

"Good lad, worthy son of a worthy father,
that upright and charitable man,
may the Lord give Heaven's blessing to you and your wife,
your father and mother-in-law.
Praise be to God that I have seen my cousin Tobias,
so like his father!"

It was later that same afternoon that Tobias tried to speak to Raguel. "Sir, you can guess how my father is counting the days till my return. I'm sure every day of my absence brings with it a fresh sorrow for both my good father and my dear mother."

"But of course," said the ebullient father-in-law. "We'll dispatch a messenger to Nineveh right away to explain everything."

"No sir! I can't let them hear of all this wonderful news from a stranger."

"That is true. No news is good news, heh?" Come; let's try some of this new wine my neighbor has brought for the occasion."

Tobias acquiesced again, thinking: 'We made good enough time, I don't suppose they'll be expecting me for a while yet.'

And so the feast continued throughout the next several days. Neighbors and relatives who had avoided the house of Raguel, for fear of his daughter, returned now with gifts and thanksgiving, prayers and praise, and music and wine; laughter and good cheer rang through the house and the whole neighborhood, and indeed, throughout the whole city of Ecbatana.

Chapter 14
Homecoming

Meanwhile, back in Nineveh, things were not so happy. Day by day Tobit had been keeping track of the time his son should have taken for his journey to Rages and back. He had allowed, in his mind, six to eight days to get there, one to get the money and rest of course, and six to eight to come back, including then two Sabbath day rests -- eighteen days in all. But, worry feeds on ignorance, and despair on worry, so within a day or two of the day he had estimated his son should have returned Tobit began to have problems.

"Perhaps he has been detained there," he said to Old Joseph. "Or perhaps Gabelus is dead and there is no one to give him the money." And as he grew anxious, ever more fearful possibilities began to occur to him, ranging from their being attacked by wild animals, bandits, evil demons, and God knows what else, until he was so upset he could no longer even pray.

Anna hadn't bothered calculating exactly when her son would return. Within a week of his leaving she was in even worse shape. Almost daily now she talked on, in a near babble, blaming Tobit for all her unhappiness as she toiled away at her loom. "My child has perished," she would say, sobbing, and sighing, "he is no longer in the land of the living -- and it is all your doing!" And she would weep, ever more piteously, as she lamented for her son: "O my child, the light of my eyes, why did I let you go?"

Tobit at first had tried to comfort her: "Hush, my dear; do not worry, he is all right. Something has happened there to distract them. The man who went with him is one of our kinsmen and can be trusted. Do not grieve for our son, my dear; he will be back soon."

"Ha! The man you sent with him claimed to be a kinsman! When Toby has claimed your money, he shows himself to be a claims man!"

"What, pray tell, is a claims man, Anna?"

"He claims the money as his own, and pushes my son over a cliff to be eaten by a mountain lion, or murdered by bandits, then off he goes to live in Babylon with the whores."

"Anna, my dear, get a hold of yourself. This would not happen."

To which she answered: "How do you know it would not happen? Be quiet and leave me alone! My boy is dead. Don't try to deceive me."

Each morning on awaking she would walk out to the main road the boy had taken, and gaze for an hour or two, neither talking nor listening to any one. Again at sunset she would repeat her sad ritual. At night she could never sleep, but wept and lamented much of the night, until, exhausted, she finally fell asleep. Then the next day on rising she would repeat the ritual again.

And each morning as the estimated time of arrival had come and then gone, old Joseph would escort Tobit to the great Caravansary where he inquired of friends and former business associates, and members of the caravans that had just arrived, if they had heard anything -- rumor, gossip, anything at all. Most replies were only a polite and sympathetic shaking of the head.

But one morning on his daily reconnoiter, the man who had rented Tobias and Azarias the donkey saw him enter the building and rushed up to him, excitedly. "Good to see you again this morning, Tobit, my friend. If you had not come today I would have had to go to your house this afternoon. Last night a caravan arrived in from Jarmo. The master of it told me there is a story going around on the mountain roads that is interesting and may give you some hope." Tobit's heart began to beat faster before even hearing the story.

Tobias and the Angel

"The caravan master who told it to me hit the road again this morning or I would have him tell it to you. Nevertheless, here is the way the story is going around among the caravan people. It seems that on the Old Smuggler's Road, high in the Zagros, not far from Jarmo...no one of any consequences uses that road anymore, at least not since the Medians have taken to patrolling the main road; the new road is much better, even though longer...I thought when we lost control, or gave up --"

"Please, my friend, tell me the story, so I may tell the boy's mother."

"Is she still taking it so badly?"

"Is she not still a mother?"

"Women! They have so little patience..."

"For heaven's sakes, friend!"

"Yes, of course, I'm sorry, now this is just the way it was told to me, so..."

"Speak!"

"Yes. Well, it seems that a band of giants attacked one of those local, inter-mountain caravans. The ones that ply the old routes, serving the smaller villages..."

"Yes?" His heart, skipping a beat, began immediately to sink. "Go on..."

"Sorry, but I wanted you to have all the details. Anyway, the master of the caravan at first tried to stand up to them. He was sure he was going to be killed. Then two men who had stopped for the night at this same rest area came and rescued them. One of them looked like a young prince, and the other one must have been his champion. The one who was the champion seemed to be a fierce warrior, and of incredible skill with a sword. The young prince was fearless too -- which is saying a lot, since most princes nowadays are a bunch of pansies. Anyway, they defeated the giants, badly wounding three of them and then driving them away.

Old Joseph took heart and nudged his master. "What do you think, sir?"

Tobit thought a moment or two. How he would love to claim the pair as Tobias and his guide, but on reflection it didn't seem possible. "I don't think it sounds too much like my son and his guide. The guide seemed a decent enough chap, forthright, confident and all, but certainly no warrior, and my son is hardly one to be taken as a prince."

Joseph inserted: "He's a fine looking boy, sir; and he has been wanting to go to officer's candidate school."

The Caravansary Master added: "Oh yes, did I mention it seems they had a wolf with them. Of course with that it began to seem like one of those mountain epics that go on and on for hours."

Joseph again: "That fellow, Azarias, did have a dog, sir."

"It was a dog alright, but certainly no wolf."

"Well, you didn't see the dog, sir."

"I couldn't see the dog!"

The man went on, "well, you know how news reports are always exaggerated. I mean they may not have been giants at all, just some of those small time bandits that prowl the foothills. But I do recall seeing a dog with the fellows when they rented my donkey. Of course, I remember it being a golden colored dog, but plenty hairy, and large enough."

Old Joseph, now supporting his master's train of thought, added, "But not so large as to be thought of as a wolf."

"Not all wolves are large," the man added, determined that he was onto something.

"And I remember him as being a friendly dog, too," Joseph added.

"I suppose you're right. But I remember the guide saying they might take the Old Smuggler's. It's faster, saves a good day or two. So that's why I thought I would pass the story on to you."

Tobias and the Angel

* * *

And back in Ecbatana, as the first week of the wedding celebration for the young couple came to an end, Raguel was well into plans for still another week. Tobias went up to his new father-in-law and said, "I must now return to my poor parents' house. I am sure they're thinking they will never see me again. I must beg you, father, to let me go now and take my beautiful bride home to my father. Remember I have already told you how I left him."

Raguel, in spite, or because, of his affability, was used to getting his own way. He said, "please, my son; stay with us just a little longer. Soon it will be that we will be separated from our dear and only daughter, to see her again only at your whim. You will know how I feel when the dear girl presents you with your own children. Please, let me send news of you to your father." And Raguel made such a good case, and his generosity was so magnanimous, that Tobias acquiesced, but again insisting that the news should come from none other than himself

"Right enough, no news is good news," Raguel reiterated, to himself, and Tobias.

When finally the next Sabbath day came, Tobias felt that same surge of strength swelling in him he had felt twice before on this journey. He went to his father-in-law again and said, quite firmly, if not emphatically, "Tomorrow we must leave here to go home to my father."

Old Raguel was about to mount another verbal assault to keep daughter and new son-in-law there, with designs already in his mind to give them this house and build another, a smaller one, for him and Edna, but looking at the lad, he suddenly felt, and looked, old. He realized he couldn't let his selfish desires alter the lives of these two that were so dear to him. He smiled and nodded. "Yes, I suppose she is yours now. Let us sit down, then, and let me spell out what it is I shall send with you."

He called for Old Jacob who came in and together the two older men went over the inventory, discussing what they would keep and what to send along, while Tobias watched in amazement. What he saw was his father-in-law giving things to him that perhaps the old man himself may need.

He interrupted them, and they looked up at him with friendly faces, "Sir," Tobias said, "we have so much already, your daughter and I. Your generosity is presenting some serious problems." The two older men looked at him as though he were a stranger, then their expressions changed to inquisitiveness, and elbowing the other, and chuckling, they went on. "Sir, my father's house, while certainly ample, will not accommodate your generosity."

Raguel looked up at him: "I guess you'll have to build a new house for my daughter, then; don't you think so, Jacob, old friend?"

"It's the very least he can do," the other man confirmed.

"I mean, if these trinkets are going to crowd them out ..."

"Exactly, sir. They'll definitely need something bigger. I mean, where will they put all those babies?"

"My point exactly!" And the two old friends continued chuckling and giving things to the young couple, marking on the papyrus sheet before him, and in the end indicating half of all that Raguel possessed. This included the male and female slaves, sheep and cattle, donkeys and camels, clothes, money and furniture. "I'm going to throw in that ugly dresser Edna keeps in the old guestroom," Raguel added with a giggle. The long list stated all that were herewith to be assigned to Tobias and Sarah.

And all the rest of the day and the next, Raguel, Edna, and servants Tobias hadn't seen, scurried around busily arranging their personal caravan to transport the young couple and their

Tobias and the Angel

new wealth back to Nineveh. The next morning Raguel, Edna, Old Jacob, Rebeccah, the cook and auxiliary mother: Even surly Kashima, who blubberingly sobbed her contrition to Sarah, bidding her former mistress the fondest goodbyes. Raguel embraced Tobias, saying, "goodbye, my son, and a safe journey to you. May the Lord of heaven give prosperity to you and Sarah your wife; and may I live to see your children." Then he turned to his daughter, Sarah, his chin quivering with his deeply felt emotion, he said: "Go to your father-in-law's house; they are now your parents as much as if you were their own daughter. Go in peace, my child; I hope to hear good news of you as long as I live." He bade them both goodbye and quickly went into the house to be alone.

Edna, however, stayed and said to Tobias: "My dear children, may the Lord bring you safely home, and may I too live long enough to see your children. In the sight of the Lord I entrust my daughter to you; do nothing to hurt her as long as you live. Go in peace, my son. From now on I am your mother and Sarah is your beloved wife. May we all be blessed with prosperity to the end of our days!" She kissed them both and saw them safely off.

Old Saul, the donkey and lion beater was at the head of the long, noisy, caravan, followed by Azarias mounted high on a gaily-festooned camel. With his right arm held high, he swung it forward, as though throwing a spear, the traditional signal for the long train to move out. They were on their way, and too soon out of the city gate of Ecbatana, heading along up the wide road that climbed to the high gorge, and on to the longer, easier, and safer, main highway to Nineveh.

* * *

The trip to Ecbatana in the first place had taken only a few days, under Azarias' able guidance. He showed his skill again on the return trip. Even with the considerably larger group than the original foursome, it was only two days later that they arrived at the junction of the Little Zab and the Tigris. Now they would avail themselves of the services of the ferry kelec across the Little Zab. The man and his son who ran the ferry service were at first happy to greet Azarias and Tobias. The boy was still at the rope helping his father. When he recognized Azarias, smiling, he kicked what had been his bad leg out and shook it, then walked ably around the deck on it. The father, without saying anything, nodded at the accomplishment to Azarias.

"We've brought a long caravan with us to collect our due. Will you still honor it?"

"Even if you had with you all the donkeys in the Zagros."

Azarias laughed, and Tobias said, "In fairness this is far more than you bargained for. We'll be giving you a bonus if you can get us all across by this afternoon."

And for the rest of the morning the caravan was taken across the little river on the ferry master's *kelec*. When the last donkey and servant came across, Azarias rewarded him with twelve silver shekels.

On their way again they were soon across the river from Assur. Soon they came upon a large inn directly across the river and which overlooked the old city, near the ferry docks, Tobias suggested this would be a good place to stop for the night.

"You're in charge," Azarias said winking at the beautiful Sarah who shared a seat on the same camel on which the rich young man was riding. And the whole caravan turned into the stopping area of the inn and unburdened the animals. Everyone in the party, including the servants, relaxed and ate dinner. After dinner, Azarias spoke with Tobias: "You know what shape your father was in when we left him?" Tobias acknowledged he

Tobias and the Angel

did. "Tomorrow morning, then, I want you to go on ahead of us, alone. Have you ridden a horse before?"

"Not really. But I can ride."

"And you're the one who wanted to go to officer's school?"

"I'll probably change my mind, now."

"I bet. Anyway, Raguel has included a fine mare among the livestock. I've had my eye on her, you may have seen her, the roan over there," and he pointed over to the corral where they had secured the animals for the night. "I think she would be good for you to learn to ride upon. So, first thing in the morning I want you to hurry on ahead to greet and comfort your parents, and see that the house is made ready before the others arrive."

"I can't do that!"

"You can't do what?"

"Leave my wife."

"Oh for crying out loud. You're not 'leaving' your wife, you're going on ahead to prepare for her. I'm staying behind to guide the caravan. I'll take care of her -- and all your riches. We'll be there probably the next day. Remember to take the fish-gall with you. Do you remember my instructions?"

"Of course."

"Tell them to me."

"The gall is now a dry powdery paste. I rub olive oil on the lids of my father's eyes. Then I spread the powdery stuff, and rub it into the oil until it makes a paste. Then I let it sit there for ... until I count to maybe one hundred. Then I peal the patches off. And he sees?"

"Not bad. Now go tell your bride what you're going to do -- just in case she might worry."

When it was dark and everybody had gone to his bed, Tobias told Sarah what he was going do in the morning. She clung to him tightly and began to weep. "What is it my precious girl?" he asked.

"First I have had to leave my dear and loving parents, now I'm going to be left behind by my loving husband. You're tired of me already. You probably have another girl in Nineveh..." and she continued to cry.

"Oh no! There has only ever been you, never, ever, another. I'm not leaving you, my adorable one. I'm just going on ahead to prepare a special place for us." She continued to sob lightly, but without much conviction he was inclined to suspect, but still, he spent the night, wooing and comforting her, and together they were able to overcome the dread of the long, the maybe even two day, separation they would have to endure.

The next morning, at first light, Tobias, and a young male servant, a boy of about twelve, an orphaned Median, who had been growing attached to Azarias, together set out for Nineveh, with Nimrod following, trotting along happily at their heels.

* * *

It was late afternoon in Nineveh, and Anna had been watching the road by which she expected her son would return. In her increasingly almost demented state, she had sat there throughout the day. And, again, as the afternoon shadows lengthened, she arose to go back home to help her husband be as miserable as she was. She stood and dusted herself off, and stared ahead one last time for the day. This time she saw something different. She had become used to the usual traffic and movement on the road. This time there was something different moving along the road toward her. Two horsemen were coming down the road at a canter, with a dog trotting along beside. Who could it be? The military rarely came on this road, local people usually used carts, and only occasionally a donkey. These were horses. This was something different. That mysterious inner knowledge, given to mothers in abundance, suddenly told her what, and who, it was. But, rather than run toward the horsemen, she ran the opposite direction to her home, not a hundred yards away, and banging inside the front door, she exclaimed loudly to Tobit: "Here he comes, your son!"

As they approached the house, Tobias said to the boy: "There it is. That's our house. You can't imagine how happy this makes me. Now I know for certain that my father's eyes will be opened."

When they reached the house and dismounted, Anna ran out the door and to him. She flung her arms around him and sobbed "here you are, my boy, my son, my life. Now I can die happy!"

"Mother, what kind of talk is that? You're not going to die at all. There are too many wonderful things in store for you and my father. Where is he?"

When Tobit heard his son's voice outside, he rose unsteadily to his feet. But before Old Joseph could get to him to aid his walking outside, he stumbled out through the front door. Tobias saw him, and fearing the old man, for he did look very old just now, was about to fall, he ran up to him and embraced him.

Then out came Old Joseph, followed by Rebeccah, and soon everybody was weeping and laughing. When things had settled down Tobias spoke softly to his father, "Father, let us go out to the courtyard. I have something wonderful for you." Together they walked through the house and back into the courtyard. Tobias sat his father down on the bench under the fig tree, and removed the fish-gall from his saddlebags. At first he was almost afraid about what he was going to do, but remembering how Azarias had healed the boy at the ferry, he went ahead with his instructions. Rebeccah was standing at the doorway to the kitchen, her head down, stealing a look at the young man with whom she was so infatuated. He talked to her, "Becky, would you bring me a cruet of olive oil, please?"

In an explosion of action she did just that, handing it to him with a curtsy. He smiled at her and her heart soared. He asked his father to put his head back and close his eyes, which the trusting, but frowning man did. Carefully Tobias poured a bit oil on each eye.

"What are you up to, son?

"You'll soon see, father." Tobias took out the glass container that Azarias had put the fish ointment in and opened it.

"What's that fishy smell?"

"You'll soon see, father."

Tobias spread the oil on his father's eyelids lavishly. Then he spread the dried, powdery, fish paste into the oil. He sat down, by his father, took him by the arm and said, "It will be all right, father."

"What will be all right? And, what are you up to, my boy. And what is that stuff, anyway. It sure stinks."

"It's fish gall. It is smelly, but it smells better now than it did, believe me."

"It sure feels funny."

"You remember the young man, Azarias, whom we hired to accompany me. He has proven to be the most remarkable friend. I watched as he healed a boy with a lame leg while on our journey. And he has given me the cure for your eyes. I have spread this powder made from dried fish gall on to your eyes. Now, if Azarias is as true as he has shown himself to be, in a short while you should be able to see."

"We'll see, or so I hope," said the father. "But, anyway, I'm so happy you've returned, Son. Life has become unbearable. I can't tell you how sad we have been. Now I know everything is going to be all right."

"Everything is going to be better than all right, father."

Now Anna came out on to the patio, escorting the boy who had accompanied Tobias. With her son home and another young male around, she was feeling almost like a young mother again. She looked at her son and husband, sitting together again under the fig tree, and for the first time in months she smiled, and felt genuinely happy, then promptly broke into sobs."

"Everything is all right, now, Mother."

"I know it is. That's why I'm crying." But she stopped crying, and looked at her husband. "What's that stuff on your father's face?"

"You'll see. Father, we are ready." And using one hand to steady his father's face, with the other Tobias gently peeled the patches that the compound had formed from the corners of Tobit's eyes. Tobit looked about. His face alighted in a smile almost too big for his face. "Praise the God of heaven! I can see."

"You can see?" Tobias asked.

"It isn't perfect, but ..." He looked long and hard at Tobias, then flung his arms round his son and burst into tears. "I can see you, my son, the light of my eyes!" he cried.

"Praise be to God, and praise to His great name,
and to all His holy angels.
May His great name rest upon us.
Praised be all the angels forever. He laid his scourge on me, and now, He has lifted it...

Look, I see my son Tobias!"

Then Rebeccah, and Joseph, brought out tasty snacks for everyone to eat, and Tobias went on to tell his father and mother about the success of his journey. He told how he had brought the money with him, and that there was so much that it was being brought in a separate caravan. Then he went on to tell about meeting their relatives, Raguel and Edna, in Ecbatana. But he said nothing yet about Sarah.

That night they enjoyed a modest feast together as a family. And Tobias, regretfully, went to bed alone. After a fitful hour or so, he finally went to sleep. The next morning he arose, early, and began determining where to build his new home, or add on to the present one. Still he said nothing to his parents about Sarah.

In the afternoon, the young lad who had been sent to help Tobias, and was showing himself to be a willing and able servant, or valet, was posted to keep an eye out for the caravan led by Azarias, and containing Tobias' treasures. It wasn't long before he came running in to announce the caravan had turned onto the street, and was heading toward their house. Tobias brought his father and mother to the patio saying he had something important to tell them.

He began without much preamble: "Mother and Father, while I was in Ecbatana, staying with our relatives there, I met and married a girl."

"You did what?" asked his father and mother, together.

"I got married."

"Married!?" the stunned father all but shouted.

A brief silence ended with, "So that's ... Why couldn't you have sent word to us?" his mother asked.

"Whom did you marry?" Tobit obviously wasn't pleased with the prospect of his son marrying outside the Klan.

"Father, Mother, my bride is Sarah, the daughter of Raguel!"

Neither parent said anything. Tobit was struck dumb. But, finally, in a weak voice he said, "Old Raggy's daughter? Son, she is -- she is, well -- (under his breath he managed to say) dangerous isn't too strong a word -- lethal is probably more accurate."

"Father," Tobias went on calmly, "she was under the spell of an evil demon, and has now been released from its grasp! She is free, and we are married! And, I am still alive."

His father was quiet. His mother looked down, then over to her husband, and again, as she had been doing increasingly, she smiled and asked, "What about a dowry, Son?"

Tobias and the Angel

Tobit said, "Old Raggy is loaded, what with all the talk about the girl, he should have been anxious to …"

"Half of all his possessions," Tobias interrupted. "But even with that, it is all of small account compared to my beautiful Sarah. And he looked over toward the door, and there was Sarah standing next to Azarias. Tobias about to burst with pride, stood and said, almost in a shout "Come my bride, and meet your other father and mother!

The two parents stood and looked together at the beautiful girl standing in the doorway. Tobit stepped forward and said, "Come in my daughter, and welcome. Praise be to God who has brought you to us. Blessings on your father, and on my son Tobias, and a blessing on you, my daughter. Come into your home and may health, blessings, and joy be yours."

And with a wonderful smile that dissolved into a sob, Anna too said, "Come in my dear, dear, daughter."

And the word spread around the Hebrew community and the day turned into a day of joy for all the Israelites living in Nineveh.

If the wedding party in Ecbatana was great, the one in Nineveh eclipsed it. For now, Tobit was nearly as wealthy as his kinsman Raguel, wealthier, for he now had his sight back, his son, a new daughter, and had earned generously from his investment in Rages.

Wealth, like manure, breeds pests. Akihar, his wife and his son, Ahnael, all came to visit. Anna, excused herself when her sister-in-law began suggesting an excellent physician to assist in assuring her new daughter-in-law a splendid, chubby, first born son.

After several days, when the marriage-feast was over, Tobit took his son aside and told him there remained only one more thing to do. "We must pay off Azarias for all his assistance, and give him something extra, over and above his wages."

"Father, how much shall I pay him? It would not hurt me to give him half of all the money he and I brought back. He has kept me safe; teaching me to fight, cured my father, my wife, and helped me bring the money. How much extra shall I pay him?"

Tobit replied, "taught you to fight?"

"Yes. Up in the mountains, he and I took on a group of bandits. With his help, and guidance, I helped to defeat them."

"Bandits? You? They weren't giants?"

"Giants? No just some scraggly looking Scythian bandits. There were five of them, but -- but the truth was, they had been drinking. Azarias really knows how to handle a sword, though. Where did you hear about giants?"

"And a wolf?" asked Tobit.

"Wolf? You mean the dog, Nimrod?"

"Not a wolf?" then Tobit shook his head in amazement, and returned to the first subject: "You're right, son. He should be given half of all that has been brought with him."

So Tobias sent for Azarias. The three gathered together in the front room of the house. Tobias said, "Azarias, my father and I have talked over the business of your pay. We feel that the amount we agreed upon before the trip should be adjusted."

Azarias smiled slyly, "Come, come, now, friends. A deal is a deal."

"That, under normal circumstances, is true. But, in view of all that you have done, and been, for all the help, wisdom, health, everything, we have decided on giving you half of all that we have brought with us. That is yours for your wages. Take it and fare you well."

Azarias looked at both men and smiled. And both men looked at Azarias, and smiled. Azarias, though, began to seem different. He said to them:

*"Praise God and thank Him before all men living
for the good He has done you,*

*So that they may sing hymns of praise to His name.
Proclaim to all the world what God has done,
and pay Him honor;
do not be slow to give Him thanks.
A king's secret ought to be kept,
but the works of God should be acknowledged publicly.
Acknowledge them, therefore, and pay Him honour.
Do good and evil shall not touch you.
Better prayer with sincerity,
and alms giving with righteousness,
than wealth with wickedness.
Better give alms than hoard up gold.
Alms giving preserves a man from death
and wipes out all sin.
Givers of alms will enjoy long life;
but sinners and wrong-doers are their own worst enemies."*

"Amen," Tobias and his father said in unison.

"Now, then," Azarias continued; "let me tell you the whole truth of the matter and bring the hidden purpose to light. When you, Tobit, were leaving your dinner untasted and burying the dead, at so great a risk, and you were praying with tears, all the while offering up those prayers, it was I who brought those prayers to the Lord, God. But, because you won his favor, trials must come to test your worth. With that testing satisfactorily completed, the great good God dispatched me, his messenger, for your healing, the deliverance of my friend, Tobias', lovely wife Sarah, and for the happy completion of these various loose ends. So, then, Who am I?"

The two men looked at each other questioningly, then back at Azarias. Tobit answered, "You are that Azarias, our kinsman, who..."

"Toby, you want to try?"

"You're not Azarias?"

"No. I am not. I am the angel, Archangel actually, Raphael. And I am one of the seven who stand in the presence of our Great Good God." Both men noticed the continuing change taking place in their friend. There was now a light on, or rather in, Azarias, or Raphael, which was becoming brighter.

Upon hearing his proclamation that he was an angel, not just an angel, but an Archangel, both men dropped down on to their knees trembling, and put their face to the ground.

Azarias, now as Raphael, continued: "It was God's will, not mine, that brought me to your side. You pay Him the thanks and praise you owe."

Tobias said, daring to look up into the splendor of he who had been his guide, and even more, his friend, said, "But -- I mean, you were with me, eating and drinking, you're the one who rescued Sarah and me from the beast... We fought together, I thought angels were, well..."

"I was at your side, eating and drinking, but only in outward show. The food, the drink I live by, man's eyes cannot see. Anyway, now's the time when I must go back to Him who sent me. This is the hard part, in more ways than one, not only leaving you, but of getting out of this mortal garb, with its limitations, and all. All the same, I have to admit it's not half bad -- all in what you get used to I suppose.

Well, then, peace be with you, now, my friends, and don't be afraid. Give thanks to God in everything, and be sure to tell the story of His great deeds. See you later, Toby." The light within and without that was becoming more and more Raphael, and evermore bright until it became a blinding light, hurting Tobias' eyes so that he had to put his head back down. Then, all of a sudden, the light dimmed again. And Tobias heard his friend say, "And Toby?"

"Yes, sir?"

"Take good care of Nimrod -- and don't forget to give him a bath. He's getting a bit smelly."

"Yes, sir."

"And…"

"Yes, sir?"

"Why don't you just go ahead and buy old Saul. Let him retire in peace."

"Yes, sir."

And with a loud rush of wind, in another moment, their friend, Azarias, aka, Raphael, was gone.

Robert Wanless

Epilogue
Rewards

Tobit lived for another forty-two years after recovering his eyesight. He lived to see his grandchildren, and his great grandchildren. Then he died quietly at the age of one hundred two.

On his deathbed, he called his son Tobias and his seven grandsons to himself. He said the following, "The Lord's words must needs come true; it will not be long before Nineveh is destroyed. After that, our exiled brethren will be able to return to the land of Israel, the deserted country. It will be populous once again, and its temple, long since destroyed by fire, will be built anew, and all those who fear God will find their way back to it.

"The Gentiles too will forsake their false gods and will take themselves to Jerusalem, and there they will find a home. All the kings of the earth will take pride in Jerusalem as they pay worship to the king who reigns in the land of Israel.

"Now you, my sons, heed well this warning of mine; do not linger in this country, but leave it as soon as you have laid your mother to rest at my side, to share my grave."

As is almost always the case of a dear and loving couple, who had shared not only life's joys but its sorrows, weathering the storms of a long marriage, as well as the more often and longer idylls, Anna, Tobias' mother, followed her dear husband to the grave only a few months later. Tobias, his wife, Sarah, his sons and their wives and their sons, Tobias' grandsons, all left Nineveh. They went for a time to live in Ecbatana, with Sarah's parents. They arrived in the city, still warm in Tobias' heart, for the wonders that had accompanied him there, and the greater wonders, which had happened there. He found Raguel and Edna, and Raguel's, servant, Jacob, thriving still. All were well content in their old age, and delighted to see the large and wonderful family descend upon them and their big empty house. Kashima now a grandmother herself, returned and joyfully tended Sarah's grandchildren, while Tobias tenderly cared for Sarah's parents. When at last Raguel and Edna died, it was Tobias who closed their eyes in death. And later when Jacob too went to join his old friend, it was Tobias that saw to the burial.

Tobias then became heir to all Raguel possessed, and himself lived to see a fresh generation yet, descendants of his own. Ninety-nine years he lived in the fear of God, and with full hearts they buried him. No kith or kin of his but persevered in uprightness and holy living; God's favor he had and man's alike, well loved by all their neighbors.

Let the story end with this prayer: Tobias had been with his father the night the good man died; a good and faithful son to the end. His father had said nothing throughout the whole afternoon. Toward sunset the old man's face seemed to become briefly young again. He opened his eyes and smiled at Tobias then raised his eyes toward heaven. With his voice as rich and smooth as it had ever been, the old gentleman spoke, offering up the following prayer:

Thou art great, O Lord, forever,
and Thy kingdom is unto all ages;
For Thou scourgest and Thou savest;
Thou leadest down to hell and bringest up again;
and there is none that can escape Thy hand.

Give glory to the Lord, ye children of Israel,
and praise Him in the sight of the Gentiles;
For this hath He scattered you among the Gentiles

who know Him not, that you may declare His wonderful works,
And that you may make them know,
that there is no other God Almighty besides Him.

He hath chastised us for our iniquities,
and He will save us for His mercy's sake.
See then what He hath done with us,
and with fear and trembling praise Him,
and in your works extol the King of endless ages!
As for me, I will praise Him in the land of my captivity,
because He hath shown His majesty toward a sinful nation.
Be converted, therefore, ye sinners,
and do justice before God,
believing that He will show His mercy unto you.
But I and my soul will rejoice in Him;
Bless ye the Lord, all His elect, keep days of joy
and sing His praise. Alleluia!

And with that prayer still on his lips, he closed his eyes in death.

Robert Wanless

Bibliography

Scripture:
The Holy Bible: Ronald Knox Translation. Sheed & Ward, New York. 1956.
The New English Bible: With the Apocrypha. Oxford University Press New York, 1971

History
The Cambridge Ancient History, Vol III, Cambridge University Press 1965
The Ancient Near East; Charles Burney. Cornell University Press Ithaca, New York 1977
The Harper Atlas of the Bible: Harper & Row, New York, 1987

Life and Times
The Might That Was Assyria: H.W.F. Saggs. Sidgwick & Jackson, London 1984
The Encyclopedia of World Costume: Doreen Yarwood, Chas. Scribner's Sons. New York, NY 1978
20,000 Years of Fashion: François Boucher. Harry N. Abrams Inc. New York, NY 1987

Geography
The Last Nomad: Wilfred Thesiger. E.P.Dutton, New York. 1980
Travelers in Ancient Lands: Louis Vaczek - Gail Buckland. New York Graphic Society. Boston.1981
Past Worlds. The Times Atlas of Archaeology: Times Books Ltd, London 1988

Robert Wanless

About the Author

Robert Wanless lives with his wife and daughter (the last of his eleven children) in Pennsylvania. There he tends his garden, bakes bread (at which he is something of an expert – three books on the subject are available) and where he reads and writes books.

Printed in Great Britain
by Amazon.co.uk, Ltd.,
Marston Gate.